Susan

(Original title: Wigwam in the City)

by BARBARA C. SMUCKER

Cover by Wayne Blickenstaff

SCHOLASTIC BOOK SERVICES

NEW YORK • TORONTO • LONDON • AUCKLAND • SYDNEY • TOKYO

ISBN 0-590-09206-5

18 17 16 15 14 13 12 11 10 9 8   2 3 4 5 6/8
                    Printed in the U.S.A.   01

To my family:
Tim, Tom, Becky, and Don

1

Susan Bearskin squashed her toes into the soft, black mud on the shore of Rice Lake. She watched her foot slowly disappear into the watery earth. If this were not such a special day, she would slip into the water and swim through the still lake. The morning mist rose about her in silent spirals like the smoke from Father's pipe.

Susan clasped her hands behind her and looked slowly around the lake. Clouds of yellow leaves trembled on the silver birches. The green pines smelled of coming winter. The tall rice grass in the shallow waters swished gently in the breeze. A pink sunrise stretched across the sky.

It was just as Grandmother Bearskin had said a few moments before as Susan watched her stir the morning campfire.

"The whole earth is ready for the Chippewa rice harvest today!"

"The whole earth is ready," Susan repeated now, "and it is the best day of the year!"

A swallow swooped from the sky and dipped into the water for a drink without breaking its flight. It rippled the water, and Susan looked down to see the reflection of her long black hair moving to and fro. The red of her calico dress and brown of her arms made zig-zig patterns in the water that caught the pink hues of the sunrise.

A shrill whistle shattered the peaceful silence.

"Jim's whistle," Susan said, as she turned quickly and started walking toward a long row of trailers and canvas wigwams. Last night most of the Indians from the Lac du Flambeau Reservation in Wisconsin had set up their camp along the banks of Rice Lake to be ready for the early morning rice harvest.

Susan's family slept in a dome-shaped canvas wigwam.

"It's not as good as a wigwam made of birchbark," Grandmother Bearskin had said when they arrived at the camp last night, "but it is better for a Chippewa to live in than a trailer made like a box."

Susan had agreed with her. But her seventeen-year-old brother Jim had not.

"A good strong trailer is better any day than an old-time wigwam," he had said.

Grandmother had shaken her head. "It is not good, Jim, that you wish for so much that is not Chippewa."

Walking slowly toward the camp now, Susan heard Jim's whistle change to a shout.

"Susan . . . come!"

Susan ran toward the camp. Everyone seemed to be awake. Dogs barked. Children laughed. English and Chippewa words of joy and excitement mingled.

When she had walked to the lake earlier this morning only the silent old people were making fires and boiling coffee. Now everyone was busy. She looked toward her family's wigwam. Jim was motioning for her to hurry. Looking at Jim beside the low wigwam, Susan realized that he was a tall, grown-up man even though he was only five years older than she. He was taller than Father.

Mother had said once that Susan and Jim got their height from their French great-grandfather. Many years before Wisconsin was a state, Great-Grandfather had traveled to America seeking furs in the north woods. He took these furs back to Europe, where they kept the fashionable lords and ladies warm in the drafty palaces of France. Some of the

French trappers who came to America married Chippewa women. Grandmother still spoke French words that she learned from her father. She had taught a few of them to Susan's father when he was a boy.

"Susan, come!" Jim's voice was impatient.

Susan was out of breath when she reached him. She sank to the ground beside Grandmother, whose full skirt circled about her as she knelt poking the crackling fire. Even though Grandmother was almost eighty she sat tall and erect. Her long gray hair, parted neatly down the middle, was pulled back from her face and braided behind and turned under, as was the custom of the old Chippewa women. Her patient black eyes, long nose, and wide laughing mouth were like Susan's. They looked more alike than Susan and Mother Bearskin, who was small and plump with light brown eyes and a dimpled smile.

"Where is Mother?" Susan asked abruptly, looking about and seeing the wigwam empty. "And Father, where is he?"

"That's why I called you, Run Away Dreamer," Jim said, not using the words with affection.

Jim's words were like a whip across her face. Susan was proud of Jim. He was the best hunter on the reservation. But lately he acted as if he didn't belong to their family. He talked about "old Indian ideas," "no jobs for Indian boys," "only white people have money." And when he said all these things he was angry and acted as if all of the Chippewa tribe were to blame.

Grandmother raised her head and spoke quietly.

"Your mother and father are with the white man from the government office." She nodded toward a large black car parked a short distance from their camp, near the highway. "The man should not have come today. White men have great impatience."

Susan looked to Jim for further explanation.

"It's about the meeting of the Tribal Council last week," Jim said. His sullen look changed to a livelier, more familiar expression. "Remember, Father told us that too many Indians are living on the reservations . . . that there would not be enough food to feed so many this winter . . . and that the men can't find jobs anywhere to earn money."

"Yes, I remember." Susan thought of Father's troubled look when he came from the Tribal Council meeting. He had spoken of Indians moving to Chicago to look for jobs. Susan had looked on the map of her seventh-grade geography book. Chicago was at the bottom of the blue dipper that was marked Lake Michigan. In the twelve years of her life, Susan had never been far away from the Lac du Flambeau Reservation. The map was just dots and names and patches of blue water.

"Father and Mother are going with that man this morning," Jim continued. "You and I must harvest the rice in our canoe."

"Oh, Jim," Susan said, startled and thrilled. "Do you think I can really do it? Mother has always been the 'knocker' in our canoe."

But Jim paid no attention to her. His eyes were on the black car, which was speeding away on the highway.

Grandmother raised her head and smiled at Susan. "You are strong and wise, Little Flower. Your mother has taught you well. It is good that our tribe should have such a young knocker to help with the harvest. Now you must eat."

Susan's uneasiness about Mother and Father left her as Grandmother's words assured her that she could do this important job. She sat on the ground beside the fire and crossed her legs under the fullness of the skirt of her red calico dress. She reached for an ear of boiled corn and quickly ate each delicious kernel. Susan knew she must hurry, but she couldn't resist tasting some hot corn meal that bubbled in a pot of beef broth over the fire.

Grandmother was now bending over their strong canoe, smoothing the edges of the thick canvas tacked on the inside. Like a stretched-out basket, the canvas would soon hold many kernels of rice that would splatter into it like tiny pellets of sleet.

"Let me help, Grandmother. What can I do?" Susan bent over the canoe, pulling and tugging at the heavy canvas.

"It's good enough now," Jim said. He looked about with impatience as many Chippewa men and women began sliding their canoes into the marshes along the bank where the tall rice grass grew.

Jim pulled their boat gently toward the water nearest them. Without waiting for anyone to tell her, Susan took her place at the head of the canoe. She carefully slid her legs under the canvas basket and firmly grasped two long sticks. With one stick she would bend the stalks of rice grass into the boat. With the other she would beat the heads of the ripe grain, loosening the kernels so they would fall into the canvas. Women always did this job and were called "knockers."

Jim stood at the other end of their boat balancing it with a long pole. Leaning on the pole, he slowly pushed their canoe through the water. Susan knew that Jim was a skillful pilot. He always missed the other boats and found the ripest grain without bruising the stalks. She hoped she could do her job as well. Susan lifted her knocking stick and waved to Grandmother, who stood proudly on the shore.

"Make a good feast, Grandmother," Susan called. She thought with happiness of the thanksgiving feast for the rice harvest that would be held this afternoon.

The mist had now disappeared from the lake and the pink sky was lighted with streaks of gold and orange. The lake shimmered with color.

Susan glanced swiftly at Jim. How could he look so bitter and unhappy on such a morning? She waited for him to give her a signal to start. Finally he nodded.

With the stick in her right hand, Susan carefully bent the stalks over the boat. Quickly she struck the heads of grain, sending sprays of rice kernels into the canvas bag. She moved from side to side, knocking the grain from the stalks on the left and then on the right. Jim's poling followed the rhythm of her sticks. The rhythm became an old Chippewa melody. Susan sang.

In the North Woods, close beside the Gitchi-Gume,
There among the pines I long to be;
The birds are singing gay,
Happy all the live-long day.

The grain filled the bag higher and higher.

"A gift from the Great Spirit." Susan thought of Grandmother's words as she watched the rice spilling into the bag with each knock of her stick.

Jim finally smiled and joined her in the song. He braced his legs against the sides of the canoe and pressed the pole deep into the rice marshes. From the opposite shore the whirr of a motorboat could be heard. Someone was not observing the rule to stay away from the rice harvesters. Waves from a motorboat could easily tip their canoe. If this happened today all the precious grain would be dumped into the muddy water. Susan dropped her sticks upon the bag of grain and grabbed the sides of the canoe. She looked toward the whirring boat. She could see a boy about the age of Jim. He wore blue swimming trunks. He was laughing with a girl in front of him. Her blond hair and white bathing suit flashed from the boat as though lit by the sun.

Jim's face became stiff and expressionless. Susan knew at once what this meant. When a white man caused trouble for a Chippewa, it was the custom to show no expression — to look aside and pretend not to notice the wrong deed. But Susan knew that Jim was angry. She knew that his hands tightened around the steering pole not just to keep the canoe steady but to express some of the anger he felt.

The canoe began to rock with the waves. Quickly Susan wrapped the canvas over the rice. If the canoe did tip perhaps she might be able to save some of the grain by holding the sack over her head. The motorboat raced toward them, churning the water into long strips of white foam.

Susan followed Jim's example and made no sound or showed no expression. She could see now that the boy in the motorboat knew the canoe was in front of him. He pointed toward them and laughed with the blond-haired girl. His boat was headed directly at Jim. Just as Susan thought he would crash into them, the boy jerked his steering stick into a turn. Water sprayed into the air. The ripples on the lake mounted into higher and higher waves. Jim gripped his pole. Susan pulled the ends of the canvas tightly over the grain. The waves slapped against the sides of the canoe. As each one hit, Jim shifted his weight from one foot to the other. When the largest one struck, the canvas bag slid to the far right of the canoe. Susan tried to lift it, but she couldn't.

"Lean to the other side, Susan," Jim shouted.

Susan obeyed at once. Jim bent his body in the same direction.

The bag of grain slid slowly back to the floor of the canoe.

The canoe jerked from side to side, but did not tip.

Jim stood erect at the bow. The splashing waves grew smaller and smaller. Susan saw the motorboat disappear through a small canal that led from Rice Lake into Lake Manitoish. They heard now only the distant putter of the motor.

"Some day I am going to be in a speedboat just like that white boy," Jim said bitterly.

Susan looked at Jim with surprise.

"It is against the laws of Wisconsin to use a speedboat for ricing. Canoes are so much better, Jim."

2

A T LAST the canvas bag was filled. Jim began poling their canoe toward the shore. Susan dipped her hands into the grain and felt the tiny kernels roll between her fingers. Her back ached and her arms felt as though they would never move up and down again, but she was happy. There was so much to show for the long hours of work.

Jim pushed back the red bandana that he wore about his head and shielded his eyes to look at the sun.

"Almost noon," he commented. "That sun must think it's still summer. It's hot enough."

He looked down at Susan and then at the filled canvas bag.

"Little Flower," he grinned, using her Chippewa

name, which he seldom did anymore. "You are one of the best and swiftest knockers on Rice Lake."

Susan said nothing in reply, but she felt like flying through the air with the swallow and dipping joyfully over the green pine forest.

Other canoes were gliding toward the shore, where friends and relatives helped them lift their loads of grain.

Susan saw Father walking toward their landing point. He was taller than the other Chippewa men and could always be seen first. Susan was glad he was back. She searched the shore for Mother and then saw her with Grandmother near their campfire.

"Jim, there's Father," Susan pointed toward the shore. "And he has new blue jeans and a new wide-brimmed straw hat."

Jim looked up quickly and waved with excitement.

Now they were near the bank. The canoe's smooth gliding halted as the boat rubbed against the miry bottom of the lake. Father reached out with his hand and caught the prow of the boat to help them land.

"Well, Little Flower," Father's eyes were focused on the filled grain canvas, "the underwater gods must have helped you, or Jim must have poled with one hand and knocked rice with the other. You couldn't get so much grain all alone."

Susan laughed. Even though Father joked about her work, she knew he was pleased. She liked the way his thick, black hair lay smooth beneath the tan brim of the new hat. She had never seen Father in new clothes. He was handsome.

Jim leaped from the boat and stood beside Father.

"Did the Relocation people give you money? Are we going to Chicago?" He stood back and surveyed Father's new clothes with satisfaction.

Susan was alarmed. She had forgotten about Chicago. And now that she remembered, she knew she had never believed that their family would move from Lac du Flambeau.

Father looked far across the lake. His black eyes expressed calm and patience. Slowly he turned to answer Jim.

"Our papers are ready. We can leave tomorrow or the next day. But first Grandmother must approve. She does not like it. She has had old Chippewa signs of unhappiness in her dreams."

"Oh, Grandmother!" Jim spoke the word bitterly. "She is a witch!" He jerked the bag of grain from the canoe and swung it over his shoulder. Then he walked away from them without waiting for an answer.

Susan was shocked. No Chippewa ever spoke this way about an old person. Old people were wise and told young people how to live. Grandmother was very wise. She was a leader among the Chippewa women.

Father put his arm about Susan's slim shoulder as they walked together toward their wigwam.

"Jim does not mean what he is saying. He has worries that you do not know about yet. And he has friends that are not good for him."

Susan couldn't talk. She felt sick inside. It was as though the shadow of the hawk spread over her, shutting out the sun and the happiness of the harvest.

A few moments ago the smell from Grandmother's kettle of boiling beef broth and corn meal had made Susan want to eat all of it. Now she couldn't swallow a spoonful. She wanted only to crawl inside the cool wigwam with Lame One, her little white dog with the crooked leg, and lie on her blanket.

"I am tired, Father, and must lie down," she said, and left him to go to the wigwam. Little plump Mother, who was always kind, came toward her.

"Little Flower, you have worked too hard. You should not do my job when you are so young."

Mother hurried inside the wigwam and smoothed Susan's blanket over the thick dry grass that covered the ground. Lame One limped toward her, wagging his tail.

Mother felt Susan's head for fever and then smiled when she found it was cool.

"Rest, Little Flower," she said to Susan as she started toward the wigwam doorway. "I must work with the rice and cook for the feast. When you are hungry the food will be warm in the kettle."

Susan nodded drowsily, rubbing the head of Lame One and feeling the thump of his tail against her arm.

She knew Mother would be busy. The rice must be dried to kill the bugs and worms; then it would be threshed to loosen the chaff from the kernels. Finally it would be tossed in the air for the wind to carry away loose chaff and bits of dirt. Susan knew that most of the rice would be sent to Minnesota in large burlap sacks, where it would be graded and packed in boxes for sale in the grocery stores. The Chippewa could keep only a small amount for themselves. Their tribe needed the money from its sales.

Tonight there would be wild rice cooked with raisins to celebrate the harvest. The Indians would come to the cleaned-off place before the Bearskins' wigwam with their cups and spoons. Father would talk, and then there would be feasting and dancing. Thinking of the feast made Susan hungry. Then she remembered Chicago and the sickness in her stomach returned.

Lame One snuggled against her and was soon asleep. Susan couldn't keep her eyes open and soon was also sleeping.

Mother looked once between the flaps of the wigwam door. She could not know that Susan's dreams were filled with the terror of a tossing canoe and a blond boy in a motorboat. Or that in her dream Chicago became a dead oak tree, creaking its black and leafless limbs in a thunderstorm.

Susan woke when the sun was setting in a red glow that matched the flames of the many campfires. There was the talk of people outside her wigwam and the laughter of many children. Lame One whined gently by her side. Susan jumped up quickly, remembering the feast and knowing that now the sickness was gone and that she was hungry enough to eat a dishpan full of rice and a dozen loaves of fried bread. Chicago couldn't be real. Grandmother had had dreams that the big city was evil. That would be the end of it.

Susan rolled her blanket tightly and placed it in the corner. She swiftly smoothed the wrinkles from her red calico dress and then ran to the tiny mirror that hung on the canvas wall. There was still enough light to see as she combed the tangles from her long black hair and tied a red band around it to hold it away from her face. Beside the mirror, Mother had placed a pan of fresh water for her to wash. Lame One wagged his tail excitedly beside her.

Outside Susan was met by her cousins Mary and Louise. They were Susan's age but were short and plump and looked like Mother. They were jolly girls with dimpled cheeks and joking eyes.

"Lazy Susan," they called to her, laughing, and then they looked at her proudly when they told her that her bag of grain was as heavy as the bags of the old ones.

Susan could think of nothing now but the hunger inside her. She laughed with her cousins and held her stomach.

"I am as hungry as a starved fox, a starved bear, and a starved lion. If the feast doesn't start soon I will eat both of you."

Now the Chippewa began to seat themselves around the cleared place before the wigwam. Susan noticed that Grandmother had placed her rush mats with the beaded centers for the old people to sit upon. Great kettles of steaming food were placed in front of them. Susan sat before her favorite dish — the wild rice and raisins. There were several kinds of meat — thin strips of dried deer meat saved from last winter's hunting, tender rabbit, and fresh fish. Delicious berry cakes, boiled in maple syrup, lay in rows on a strip of birch bark. Flat bread sizzled in frying pans over hot coals.

The old people said that the totems of everyone present could be pleased only by serving its meat. Susan, Jim, and even Father, didn't believe much in totems. But they knew their meaning and that Chippewa of Grandmother's age believed that all men had a close bond with animals. In ancient times each family took a symbol representing either a bird, a mammal, a fish, or a reptile. Some of the people wore the teeth or claws of their animal totems. The Chippewa's favorite totems were the bear, the wolf, the catfish, and the duck. Children always inherited their totem from their father. Susan and Jim belonged to none of the favorite totems. Their totem was the lion. This was because their great-grandfather was a Frenchman. He had had no totem to pass down to his children, until one day a Chippewa saw the picture of a lion on the French coat-of-arms. It was decided immediately that the lion would be the totem of all Chippewa children whose fathers were French.

All Susan's relatives on Father's side of the family were members of the lion totem. It was a good way to know members of your own family. Susan and Jim did not believe that the totems were sacred, but they did believe it their duty to conserve the totems. If the totem was a fish, the Chippewa of that totem must see that fish were not wasted and that people did not kill so many that they could not multiply.

Father stood at the head of the circle of Chippewa. Obeying an old custom, he shook tobacco into the nearby fire as an offering to the Great Spirit, Manito.

Then he spoke simply, "I suppose you know why all this food is given to us. It is a gift of the Great Spirit from the earth. Let us give thanks for this food we are going to eat."

Susan thought how handsome Father looked in his new blue jeans and red plaid shirt. The firelight gave his dark skin a red glow and made his eyes burn as bright and strong as those of the lion.

All the Chippewa were silent as Father continued with an old Chippewa thanksgiving prayer: "Now is the season of harvesting things. Now we give thanks to our Creator. Now we sprinkle tobacco on the fire. Now smoke arises; it lifts our words to Him. Now we speak to Manito, the great ruler, the great life, one Great Spirit."

All the happiness of the day returned to Susan — the rhythm of the rice harvest — the lingering warmth of summer. Surely Father would never want to leave all their friends and relatives. How would it be possible to go away from the rice marshes, the great round lake, and the green pine forests?

Darkness spread over the campgrounds while everyone ate. The campfires grew brighter. Fireflies blinked off and on above the grass and around the trees. Little children shouted and raced after them. Susan and her cousins carried pans and cups from the clearing. It was the time now for the dancing.

Old Eaglefeathers and Father put on their ceremonial head feathers and walked to the center of the clearing with their drums. Old Eaglefeathers was the leader of the drum songs and always sang in a high trembling voice. He and Father beat the rhythm together. Jim was the best of the young singers. Susan hoped that he might become leader of the songs.

Susan looked quickly about the group. Where was Jim? Mother and Grandmother were cleaning the pans and putting them in order. Cousin Mary sat beside a log near the campfire pulling on her newly beaded moccasins. Louise sat beside her smoothing her black hair beneath a red headband.

The older boys talked and smoked in the shadows of the birches. No one was walking near the lake. Everyone stood close by, for they could hear Father and Old Eaglefeathers tapping on their drums to test the tightness of the deerskin covers.

Maybe Jim had gone inside the wigwam. Susan ran to the open door and looked inside. It was empty. The cooking pots were stacked in neat piles beside the rolls of blankets. Jim's boots were near his blanket and the blue jeans he wore while they were ricing hung over a hook on the side wall. His blue nylon jacket was missing. Why would he want a jacket now? The air was still warm from the daytime sun. The coolness had not risen yet from the lake water. Susan was worried. Jim's strange anger the past few months made him do things that no one expected.

The rhythmic beat of the drums filled the wigwam like a summons. The sound always excited Susan. She could never hear the drums without wanting to run to them and enter the dances — following the rhythm with the beat of her feet and swinging her body to the song of the high-voiced singer. Quickly she grabbed her gourd rattle, which was filled with pebbles, and slipped her feet into the soft smoothness of the new moccasins Father had made for her. She raced outside to the firelight and the beating drums.

Old Eaglefeathers was singing the song for the Deer Dance.

This dance was a favorite of all the Chippewa. Susan and Jim had often heard the story of the Chippewa hunter who long ago woke from his sleep to the sound of drums. He ran through the forest in search of them and found to his amazement a large group of deer facing one another. They were dancing and rubbing their horns together and the sound this made was like that of beating drums.

When the Chippewa men did the Deer Dance they pretended they were deer. They faced one another and locked horns and danced as though they were in battle. Their feet kept perfect time to the drumbeat as they tossed their feathered heads and dodged back and forth to miss the horny thrusts. The women and girls crossed back and forth between them, never losing a step and never stopping the rhythm.

Susan found her place behind Mother and stomped her feet inside the soft, noiseless moccasins. Father and Wild Deer beat the drums faster and faster. Eaglefeathers raised his high clear voice in the call of battle. Heads lowered and struck and then struck again. All the women and girls swayed together as one person. Susan's feet rose and fell as though she no longer controlled their movement. She felt excited and joyous and close to her relatives and friends and to all the ancient ways and beliefs of the Chippewa people.

The drumbeats grew slower and softer. The men lifted their heads. The imaginary battle of the deer was ending. The women and girls danced from the circle, humming and laughing.

The sound of strange footsteps turned the attention of everyone from the fire to the path leading from the road. To their surprise and astonishment, a policeman in a blue uniform walked into the light of the campfire. He seemed equally astonished, but soon stiffened and pulled a white card from his pocket. Looking down at it closely and then at the silent Chippewa gathered around him, he asked, "Is there a Mr. Bearskin here? I'm looking for the father of Jim Bearskin."

The warmth of the dance left Susan. She felt as though she were standing in a pool of icy water. She moved close to Father and walked with him to the circle of firelight where the policeman stood.

"I am Mr. Bearskin," Father said hesitatingly.

The policeman looked down again at the card.

"Your son has been arrested for riding in a stolen car," he said. "You must come with me to the police station in Manitoish."

3

FATHER invited the policeman to come inside their wigwam. But he shook his head impatiently.

"There's no need for more talk," he said. "Just come to the police station, Bearskin."

"I have no car," Father answered simply. "There are just the wagon and horse here to take us back home."

The policeman walked back and forth and checked several times on his wristwatch. Susan thought of Grandmother's words that white men are always in a hurry and are always pushing to go somewhere.

"I guess you'd better come with me," the policeman said, pulling a long flashlight from his pocket. He swung the circle of yellow light around the wigwam and into the faces of the silent Chippewa in the dance circle. Then he flashed it up and down the path between the silver birch trees.

"Let's go," he called and started walking.

Father turned to Mother and Grandmother.

"You will have to ask the Uncles to help you pack. Go home tonight. I will come there."

No one noticed Susan, so she quietly walked behind Father. The round ball of light bounced in front of them, but it did not touch the black night where Susan walked. No one spoke. There was just the pounding crunch of the policeman's boots on the ground and the cracking of branches as he pushed them aside with the swing of his arm. The moccasins which Susan and Father wore were as silent as rabbits' paws.

Once an owl's quivering screech stopped their walking.

The policeman threw his light into the tree and aimed a rock at the solemn bird. "Get!" he shouted.

The great bird flapped its wings and flew into a higher branch, where it screeched again. Susan was glad it was safe. Owl-of-the-Night, Grandmother told her once, stayed awake to guard the night creatures from harm. He was a wise and good friend.

Soon the light focused on a black police car with a red light on the top of it. The policeman walked toward it and unlocked the car door. He motioned for Father to get inside. Then he saw Susan.

"Who's this kid?" he asked. "She shouldn't be coming along."

"She is my daughter," Father said with no expression of surprise. "She will not bother us. It is too dark for her to go back to the camp alone."

The policeman shrugged his shoulders.

During the long, dark car ride there were no words spoken. Susan held Father's hand. It was cold and tense. She looked out the window and saw the black pine trees outlined against the sky like the pointed ears of many foxes. Their friendly, green warmth had disappeared with the night and they were stiff and frightening.

Susan began to think of Jim. There must be a mistake. Jim would never steal a car. What could they do with him in a police station? Susan had heard stories of jails where people were locked in small rooms and never allowed to walk out-of-doors. How could strong Jim, who liked to hunt and fish, stand such a thing? She could not ask Father her questions. He would never talk before the policeman.

The lights of the town could now be seen dotting the night like giant fireflies. Susan had been in Manitoish only once before and that was to meet the bus which brought Uncle John Drumbeater from Oklahoma, where he was studying in a college to be a teacher. Uncle John was Mother's brother and he was the only Chippewa on the Lac du Flambeau Reservation who studied in a college.

The police car stopped before a square building with brightly lighted windows. Susan's heart thumped like drums for a war dance. She looked to see if there were bars of steel across the windows. But they were only dusty and splattered with summer bugs. She followed Father and the policeman inside the building. They entered a small room with the smell of an old, haunted house. The policeman opened another door. This one took them into a wide, open room with rows of empty benches. Susan saw Jim! He was sitting on a bench at the front of the room with two other Chippewa boys. Their heads were bowed and their shoulders slumped like the backs of timid beavers. Jim didn't look up. In this great room he was just a small boy. This morning he had been taller than the wigwam, and in the boat he had stood straight and proud as the deer.

There were other Indian parents in the room and Susan and Father were told to join them. None of them spoke. They looked straight ahead at an old white-haired man who sat above them behind a tall wooden desk.

"He is the one who will tell us what will happen to Jim," Susan thought, and she trembled.

The old man leaned on the desk, moving his thick glasses up and down the slope of his nose. He peered at the parents and then at the boys. Susan tried to hide behind Father to avoid his staring.

The white-haired man cleared his throat and began to talk. His tired voice shook. Susan was surprised. His voice was like Old Eaglefeathers', who sang to-night for the Deer Dance. It was worn with use but it was kind. It made her feel safer about Jim.

"I guess you parents and boys know why you are here." He paused for a long time, staring again at the parents and then at the boys.

Susan's heart pounded. Her throat was too dry to swallow. Would he talk about Jim now?

He turned his face toward the parents. "Your boys wanted to take a ride. One of them, Ray Martin, broke into a garage and took a car. This is the third car he has stolen. I'm afraid this time we will have to send him to the State School for Boys at Waukesha."

Susan's knees shook. She wondered if she would be able to stand. She had heard stories about the State School, where the windows were barred and boys were locked in their rooms at night. Would Jim go too? She reached for Father's hand. It was cold and trembling.

The old man looked at the three boys. "Jim Bear-skin and John Otter didn't know the car had been sto-len. They went along for the ride."

Neither Jim nor his friend lifted their heads.

"These boys seem to be good boys," he went on, "but they quit school at sixteen and there's nothing for them to do. They see you fathers out of work and it's a bad influence."

Susan stepped forward. She would tell this man that Father and Jim had tried and tried to find jobs. She would tell him that Father had taught Jim to be the finest hunter on the reservation.

Father grabbed her by the shoulder and pulled her back. He bent down and whispered in Chippewa, "Don't be a mule-head. At this place you must not be the speaker like your grandmother. Be silent like your mother."

Susan moved behind Father. Would she really have spoken in this great room? Was she a mule-head?

The old man swayed back and forth in his chair, stroking his chin.

Susan held her breath. Now he would surely tell them what would happen to Jim.

"Take the two boys home now," his voice trembled, "and don't let them get mixed up with the wrong kind of friends again."

Father squeezed Susan's hand. She was weak and her hand shook.

The same policeman who brought them tapped Father on the shoulder and motioned for him to follow.

Jim was waiting for them at the door. He was like Lame One, who wouldn't look up after he had been punished.

The silence of a fishing trip filled the car. Outside, a rising wind swished against the windows, and a fine, cold rain splashed angrily in broken puddles against the glass. The beautiful day of the rice harvest was washed away.

Several times lightning streaked the sky and lighted the faces of those in the car. Susan glanced at Jim. His face was angry and his eyes snapped with contempt.

The police car slowed down as it neared a group of small tar-paper shacks. Dim lights from coal oil lamps flickered from the windows.

"Which one is yours?" The policeman startled Susan by speaking.

"We are at home," Susan realized with surprise. She had forgotten that Father said they would not return to Rice Lake.

Father answered the policeman quietly, "The house at the end of the road."

Susan was relieved when she saw lights in the windows of their house. It meant that Mother and Grandmother were home from Rice Lake and that they would have a wood fire started in the cooking stove. She shivered. Her worn red calico dress felt thin and skimpy.

The police car stopped at the end of the road. Father opened the side door and Susan slid out. Jim followed.

The policeman turned to Jim. "You better listen to that judge and stay out of trouble." Jim hunched his shoulders and ran for the door of their house.

"Thank you for bringing us home," Father said before closing the car door. His lips were straight and his eyes had no expression.

Susan ran after Jim. Mother opened the door. She was smiling. She pointed to the bench beside the table.

"Uncle John Drumbeater!" Susan cried, and ran into his outstretched arms.

Jim smiled too and shook Uncle John's hand.

It was good to have him here. It meant that they would not talk about Jim and the stolen car until tomorrow. They would listen to Uncle John tell stories of his college and of the people in Oklahoma.

The rain pounded in drumbeats against the tarpaper walls. Water leaked through the roof and rolled into balls of dust on the hard dirt floor. Mother frowned and placed pans beneath the largest puddles. Susan knew that a muddy floor would be cold under her blanket bed tonight. In the two-roomed Bearskin home there were only one bed and a small cot. Susan and Jim always slept on the floor.

The dripping rain stung the metal of the pans.

Susan hated the sound. It meant the coming of winter — the cold walks with frozen pails of water from the well, the tight coat and leaky shoes for school, the sickness that came to Mother and made her lie in bed with coughing and a fever.

Thoughts of winter filled the room until Grandmother shook the smoking stove. Bright tongues of fire rose from the burning wood and filled the room with light and warmth. The flames licked against a kettle of leftover soup, changing the dampness to the delicious fragrance of deer meat and wild rice. Mother placed a dish of blueberry cakes on the table. Susan nodded sleepily and leaned against her blanket roll. She was ready for the stories of Uncle John.

But he had only a question. "When do you go to Chicago?" he asked.

Susan blinked her eyes and jumped to her feet. Had she been asleep? Was she dreaming? She looked at Father.

He leaned across the table toward Uncle John. His long brown fingers clasped together in front of him. In the gleaming firelight his troubled eyes looked moist.

"We have not had time to tell the children." He nodded at Susan and then at Jim. "Mother and I signed the papers at the Relocation Office this morning. We will go to Chicago on the train day after tomorrow."

It had happened! The bad dream had come true. Wouldn't Grandmother stop them? Chippewa always obeyed the old people, for they were wise and knew about the future. But Susan could see that Grandmother knew and that she had said yes to the move.

They were going to leave their home and the reservation. She had seen only two pictures of Chicago in the Relocation Office. In one of them an Indian mother stood between a television set and a great white refrigerator. In another, there were rows of tall white buildings poking up around the edge of a great blue lake. Susan had never seen a television or a refrigerator. She didn't want either of them. And she didn't like buildings around a blue lake. She liked tall pine trees and thin silver birches.

4

Susan shivered inside her blanket roll. The hard, dirt floor beneath her was no longer warm with summer. When winter came it would be a brick of ice. With half-closed eyes, Susan reached forward to wrap the blanket more tightly about her. A bright beam of sunlight struck her face. It was morning!

Susan looked about the room. It was empty. Not even Lame One was at home. A thin ribbon of smoke rose from the wood-burning stove and a pan of food warmed on the top of it. On most mornings like this, Susan would have crawled back inside the blanket and gone to sleep again. Yesterday she had worked hard. Today she could rest. It wouldn't matter that her family had left the house. Why shouldn't they?

The sun was shining. Father might think it a good time to fish.

But today was different. All the events of the night before pressed around her. She remembered . . . Jim, bent like a beaten dog in the big courthouse . . . the silent policeman in the racing black car with the red light that looked into secret places . . . the dripping cold shack that held misery in the winter . . . the joy of finding Uncle John Drumbeater . . . the great, dark fear of leaving home and moving to Chicago.

Susan shivered again. It would be warm out-of-doors in the sun. The little fire in the cooking stove held no heat. Mother must have known she would be cold. On the chair beside the table hung her gray winter skirt and the faded blue sweater. Susan quickly put them on and ran out-of-doors. The air was sweet and fresh with the smell of ripened harvests. Last night's problems began to disappear. Then she saw Uncle John sitting beneath the large birch tree, reading a book.

"Little Flower," Uncle John looked up. "I thought you would sleep around the sun. I've almost finished this book, waiting for you."

Susan laughed.

"And I'm hungry," Uncle John continued, "I think there's something warm on the stove that we can eat out here."

Susan was hungry too. She returned to the stove

and found that the warm food was wild rice and raisins left from the harvest feast. She filled a bowl for Uncle John and one for herself.

Uncle John found a dry log and rolled it near the tree. The ground was wet with last night's rain, and pools of water made little mirrors in all the hollows. A fat robin dipped its beak in one of them. Susan laughed again. Birds took such fast drinks and then bobbed their heads about as though afraid of being watched.

"Little Flower, I have all morning to tell stories or just talk with you," Uncle John said, reaching for the bowl of food that Susan offered. "Your mother and grandmother have gone to the store to buy clothes for your trip tomorrow. Your father and Jim are meeting with the Tribal Council. Maybe we should fish. . . . Or, maybe we could kill a rabbit for dinner. Which shall it be? You choose."

Susan knew at once what she wanted to do. Uncle John must be the one to stop their moving to Chicago. Father would listen to him because he was wise and read many books and studied in a college.

There were no reasons at all why she should hide her feelings from Uncle John. He had always been her friend.

Susan placed her bowl of rice on the ground near his and stood impatiently in front of him.

"Uncle John, you must help me." Her eyes filled

with tears but she quickly wiped them away with the sleeve of her sweater.

"I don't want to go to Chicago tomorrow. I don't want to leave Lac du Flambeau. Cousin Mary's father says Chicago is like a dark prison. Mary couldn't breathe there. There is cement all over the ground, so the grass has no place to grow. Uncle John, you must tell Father and Mother that it is wrong. . . ."

Susan stopped talking. She could see that Uncle John did not agree.

"I won't go!" Susan stomped her foot defiantly.

"You are a mule-head," Uncle John became stern. "There are times for you to talk, Susan, and there are times for you to listen. Now, sit on that log and hear what I have to say."

Susan was amazed. Uncle John usually joked about her stubbornness. He was not joking now. His round face was creased with downward wrinkles. His black eyes narrowed.

"Our people today do not know enough about their past, Susan," Uncle John said. "They do not know why they are poor and why they cannot find jobs. They must think each day how to get enough food to keep from starving in the winter."

"But you have heard Grandmother say that Lac du Flambeau is the best place in the world to be poor," Susan interrupted.

"I don't think the Chippewa have to be poor, Susan."

Susan was puzzled. What could they do? Hadn't Father and Jim looked for jobs?

Uncle John gripped the tree log tightly with his hands and talked in a voice that was harsh and bitter.

"Indians who want to live on the reservations must be allowed to build shops and factories on them so they can have jobs at home. Our tribes must be allowed to run these industries and to own them. We must learn to be noble and independent people again."

"I don't understand," Susan cried, confused and worried that Uncle John should speak in such anger.

"I'm sorry, Little Flower," Uncle John said, and smiled. The harshness and anger left his face. He paused for a long time and then said, "I have learned from many books, Susan, that our ancestors came to this country almost twenty thousand years ago. They were hunting people and they traveled to every part of this great land. Our tribe came to Wisconsin centuries before the state had a name. They liked the green forests, the deer, the red berries, the maple trees, and the wild rice."

Susan was fascinated. Twenty thousand years! It was hard to think of a thousand or even a hundred.

Uncle John went on: "After many years white men

came. At first they were friends of the Indians. Each group learned new ideas from the other. Then more and more white people came. There were wars. The white settlers wanted the land."

Susan interrupted. "There is so much land," Susan swung her arms around her as though embracing the entire forest. "Couldn't everyone find a place to live?"

"There might have been room, Susan," Uncle John answered, "but the white men believed they could buy the land with money and then own it so that no one else could hunt or fish upon it again. The Indians had nothing in writing which said the land was their home. Some of the new settlers looked upon our ancestors as wild beasts who roamed about and needed to be wiped out."

Uncle John paused and gazed thoughtfully at the silent row of strong pine trees with their green needles glistening in the bright sun.

"The Indians didn't understand about buying land. For thousands of years we have believed that the Great Spirit gave us the land to use, but not to own. Our tribe and our people are part of all nature. Each family cannot own little squares of it. We must try to live in harmony with nature."

Susan understood. Uncle John started to speak again when a crashing noise sounded in the woods behind the Bearskin home.

Could it be a bear or a deer running from a hunter? Susan turned around quickly. The cracking branches and the measured steps on the dry leaves sounded more like a man. He was taking a shortcut to the Bearskin shack and was avoiding the winding path that led through the woods.

The tangled raspberry bushes behind Susan and Uncle John parted. It was Jim.

He stopped for a moment in front of them, gasping for breath. His shirt was torn from the shrubs and branches and his face was wet with perspiration.

"Jim!" Susan ran toward him.

He looked at the house.

"Is anyone in there?" he managed to ask, still breathing heavily.

"No one is at home, Jim, but Susan and me," Uncle John answered.

Jim raced inside the shack and returned in a few minutes carrying his jacket and a blanket roll.

He stopped in front of them and then turned as though listening for following footsteps in the woods.

"I have to go away." His eyes pleaded with Uncle John and Susan but his voice was harsh. "There isn't time to tell you why."

"Do you have money?" Uncle John asked.

Jim sneered. "That's a funny question, Uncle John. Does a Chippewa ever have any money?"

Uncle John said nothing but reached inside his

jacket and pulled out a leather wallet decorated with brightly colored beads. He opened it and took out a five-dollar bill.

"This isn't much. But it's all I have. Take it, Jim, and remember that you and I are Chippewa. We help each other when we can."

Jim hesitated and then reached for the bill. He folded it and put it carefully inside his trouser pocket.

"I've never had so much money," he said. "Thanks, Uncle John."

He turned toward Susan and gave her a sudden smile, "Good-bye, Little Flower."

The distant noise of an approaching car interrupted them.

Jim stiffened. He glanced nervously down the road at the oncoming car. His expression became bitter and determined. Quickly he tied his jacket around the rolled blanket and slung it over his shoulder. Without another word he ran into the woods.

Susan started to follow him, but Uncle John grabbed her hand and held it tightly.

"He wants to leave Lac du Flambeau, Susan. It isn't good to run away, but Jim must learn this for himself."

Susan was confused. Surely the Tribal Council wouldn't punish Jim severely. The white judge said he wasn't guilty. Why should he want to run away. Why did he look so bitter before he left. Was it because he couldn't find a job? Was it because he worked one day on a road-building crew, until the foreman saw him and yelled, "Who hired this Indian? I won't have a lazy Indian on my crew."

Susan thought about that day. She knew some Chippewa who were lazy — like Slow Pace and his brother. But Jim and Father were not lazy. They were good fishermen. They could make fine moccasins when they had leather. They were the best hunters on Lac du Flambeau.

Susan looked toward the oncoming car and then into the woods where Jim had disappeared. There were no waving branches to tell the path he had taken.

Maybe, Susan thought hopefully, Jim will camp in the woods for the night and come home in the morning.

Then she remembered their family would not be at home. Tomorrow they were going to Chicago! How would Jim find them?

"Uncle John," Susan pleaded, "we must find Jim. We can't go to Chicago without him."

Uncle John spoke with impatience. "You are going to Chicago tomorrow because that is the only place your father can find a job. If he doesn't work, you, and your mother, and your grandmother will not have enough to eat this winter. Your mother will be sick if she has to spend another winter in that shack."

Susan was surprised. No one had spoken so urgently to her about moving.

"And another thing, Susan," Uncle John continued. "Maybe in Chicago you will have shoes and a coat so you can go to school all winter."

It was hard to think about winter when the sun spread over them now as warm as an Indian blanket. But Uncle John was right; she often stayed away from school in the winter because her shoes had cracks in the sides and holes in the bottom.

The car which had frightened Jim drove slowly by the cabin. It was filled with strangers. Susan had expected Father and other men of the Council and perhaps even a policeman. She was relieved.

Now she heard the clopping hooves of a horse and the creaking wheels of a wagon. It was Mother and Grandmother. She must tell them about Jim. She raced down the road to meet them.

5

Swirls of dust gathered in the clearing before the Bearskin home. Father and Striking Thunder strode from the path in the woods toward Uncle John, wiping their faces with red bandanas.

Mother's wagon bumped into the clearing as Susan joined her.

"It's Jim," Susan managed to shout to Mother and Grandmother above the creaking of the wagon wheels and the snorting of the horse, "he's run away."

Mother's round face widened with alarm. She yanked the reins and halted the slow-moving horse. Handing the reins to Grandmother, she climbed over the wagon's side, flinging her full skirt in front of her. She grabbed Susan's hand and together they walked to the tree where Father stood with Uncle John and Striking Thunder.

Grandmother rose in the wagon, holding the reins before her. Her strong, resonant voice sang through the air.

"Tell us at once, John, what has happened." She sensed that Uncle John knew the answer.

The others were silent. Grandmother was the oldest one present. Susan knew that she should speak first. Her age gave her wisdom.

Father was impatient. "Tell us which way he ran, John. The Council thinks Jim should stay on Lac du Flambeau another year."

"Another year!" Susan cupped her hand over her mouth to silence her rejoicing.

A gentle smile appeared on Uncle John's jovial face. "Jim has been running in the woods for many minutes. To chase him now would be like catching that squirrel in the tall pine with bare hands."

He told all of them about Jim's leaving with his blanket, and about the five-dollar bill.

"He can't accept the poverty of the reservation," Uncle John spoke solemnly. "He wants a car, a motorboat, new clothes, and all the things he sees outside the reservation."

Grandmother cleared her throat from her high place in the wagon.

"The boy often sleeps in the woods overnight," she said. "He will come home in the morning."

This settled the problem for Grandmother. She had other jobs to do. She called for Susan to help lift some heavy brown packages from a corner of the wagon.

Susan was usually obedient to Grandmother's opinions as well as to her requests. But this time she doubted Grandmother's wisdom about Jim. She walked thoughtfully to the wagon. Grandmother stood above her with her arms loaded with packages. They were all sizes! Susan reached for one of the bundles and saw "Dress Shop" printed on the cover.

New clothes! she thought. She remembered. Mother had bought them with money from the Relocation Office. All Indians were given clothes money when they left the reservation. If these are new clothes, Susan thought as she clasped her hands tightly around the packages, I will have to send them back if we don't go to Chicago. She pressed one of them close to her eyes and tried to see through the brown paper.

Susan had never had a new dress or a new pair of shoes. Maybe Mother would let her open the packages even if they were to be taken back to the store.

From the open door of the shack, Susan heard Father talking. Mother stood beside him with bowed head, weeping silently. Susan wanted to help. She had never seen Mother cry. She felt torn into two people. Part of her wanted to cry with Mother, and part of her wanted to shout with excitement about the packages. She saw Father standing close beside Mother. His usual calm voice was tense and high-pitched.

"Jim was quiet when the Council meeting started," he told Mother and Uncle John. "Then Striking Thunder here said our family should stay on the reservation another year and keep Jim with us. He said Jim was not learning the ways of the Chippewa. When Jim heard this, he jumped from the bench and ran out the door."

Striking Thunder affirmed Father's story by nodding his head and saying, "Yes, yes."

Father took the new straw hat from his head and wiped his forehead. He put it carefully on the ground beside Uncle John.

"Did anyone try to stop him?" Uncle John asked.

"We thought he would come back," Father answered.

There was a short silence.

"I am worried now about the five dollars," Susan heard Father say. "Jim might buy a bus ticket and think it will be enough to take him to Chicago."

"He will get to Chicago if he has to walk," Uncle John answered, looking toward the silent green forest where Jim had disappeared a few moments before.

50

"The boy has new ideas in his head. There is no room for the ways of the Chippewa."

Susan was shocked. How could Uncle John talk in such a way? Grandmother was older and wiser. She should know best.

Father built a fire and the men pulled logs around it. Their voices became a mumble and Susan could no longer hear the words. Mother walked slowly to the house, wiping her eyes with the hem of her full skirt. Her shoulders drooped. Strands of black hair fell from the neat part down the middle of her head. She didn't bother to push them in place.

"Jim will sleep in the woods tonight and come back tomorrow," Susan spoke cheerfully, trying to comfort Mother. But the words were like bubbles with nothing inside. Susan knew they might not be true.

Grandmother lifted the lid from a kettle and clamped it down briskly. This was her sign that enough had been spoken about Jim.

"Susan is right," she said with finality. "Jim will come home. He is only a boy who is trying to be a man."

Susan bent over the table, unable to stay away from the packages.

"Do you think I could open the paper and look at the clothes?" Susan asked Mother. "I won't touch them in case we take them back to the store."

Mother agreed.

"Why don't you try this one first," she said, and handed a middle-sized package to Susan.

Susan tingled with excitement. It was the way she felt the day she looked into a robin's nest and saw a baby bird pushing itself out of an egg shell.

As she carefully unfolded the brown paper it made a crackling sound. Inside was a new dress! Susan's eyes sparkled.

"It has yellow daisies all over it," she said softly. The cloth was fresh and springy. It was like the new dresses she had seen white girls wear on the streets of Manitoish.

Mother's face dimpled with smiles. She handed Susan a large, heavy package.

There was a tight string around this one. Susan wanted to bite the stubborn knots that bound it. Grandmother cut them expertly with a sharp kitchen knife. The package burst open. Inside was a soft, blue coat!

"Like a patch of blue from the sky," Susan whispered, and pushed it close beside the daisy-covered dress.

Grandmother shook her head, drawing away from the table. "It is not good for one girl to have so much."

Susan hesitated before she reached for the next

package. She did not want to oppose Grandmother, but how could she stop the excitement inside her.

Mother answered quietly, "It is only what we need if we move to the city."

Mother placed a third package in front of Susan. It was a smooth, white box. Susan lifted the lid. White tissue paper popped up like bubbling foam from a bottle of pop. Beneath the paper was a pair of new black shoes. They shone like the wings of a blackbird. The soles were strong and thick.

"Water could never soak through these," Susan said, as she turned the shoes over and rubbed her finger over the smooth, hard surface.

"I promised not to touch anything," she reminded herself, pushing the shoes into the white tissue and sliding the lid over the box.

Susan became angry. Why do I have to go to Chicago to have these clothes? she thought. With such heavy shoes I would never miss one day of school on Lac du Flambeau. The blue coat would be warm in the frozen winter.

She wanted to put all the clothes on and show them to Father and Uncle John, but more than this she wanted to stay at home.

"I won't wear any of these clothes," Susan said, and turned away from the table. "Besides, it is better for the Chippewa to give gifts than to receive so many for themselves."

Grandmother smiled. "You are a stubborn child, Little Flower, and a Chippewa in your heart. This will not change even though you live in the city."

Susan stood in the open doorway. The afternoon sun streaked over the top of the pine forest, covering the front of the Bearskin shack with an orange-gold light. Its noontime warmth was gone, but the glitter of yellow birch leaves and the friendly smoke from the fire inside the circle where the men talked held warmth. Susan forgot the clothes. If only Jim would come back from the forest beyond the sunlight where it was already getting dark.

The men left the fire and began to scatter along the road. Uncle John went with them. Father walked toward the house.

"Tomorrow we will go to Chicago," he announced when he entered the door. "It is best that we carry out our plans."

Susan was alarmed. "What about Jim, Father? We can't go without him."

Father sat on the floor close to the cooking stove and crossed his legs in front of him. He sat like this when there were serious matters to tell the family. Susan moved close beside him.

"Jim will come home when he learns that five dollars is like a drop of water in a dry cornfield." Father lit his pipe and puffed slow, lazy circles of smoke. "When he comes back he will stay with Grandmother."

"Will Grandmother stay here?" Susan asked, startled. How could they go without Grandmother? She was part of their family as much as Jim. She thought of Jim alone in the dark woods as she listened to snatches of Father's conversation.

"Jim can guide hunters and fishermen on Lac du Flambeau until winter," Father told the family. "There is no other job for him here. If Jim had listened to the Council and not run away, all of us would have stayed for another winter."

If Jim had not run away . . . the family might stay! Susan repeated the words to herself. Could she have heard right? An idea began spinning in her head.

She must find Jim and bring him home tonight. Father and the men of the Council said he would come home. But Susan knew he could live many days in the forest. There were blueberries and wild rice to eat. He could shoot squirrels and rabbits with a bow and arrow, which he knew how to make.

Susan knew where he would camp. He would go to their secret hiding place — the Tallest Pine. Jim and she had rested there one afternoon when they were hunting wild raspberries and became lost. Its straight black trunk pushed its way above all the other trees, until its branches spread and stretched over the forest like the eagle's wings.

Tonight, when everyone was sleeping, she would go to the Tallest Pine. She would take Lame One with her. It would not be dark. The moon was bright and round for the harvest. She wondered if she should tell Uncle John. He might go with her. Then she remembered how he said Jim would not come home and that Jim wanted to forget he was a Chippewa.

6

As THE LIGHT OF DAY left the sky, a pumpkin-orange moon rose over the horizon. It puffed itself larger and larger until it became a round lamp in the sky, spreading a green-white light through the forest.

Susan rolled into her blanket on the hard floor and turned her face toward the wall. She must only pretend to sleep.

Lame One snuggled against her back. Susan listened with open eyes. At last Father blew out the flame on the lamp. The cot on which Grandmother slept squeaked and then was silent. Grandmother was asleep. Whispers could be heard from Mother and Father about trains and tickets and Jim. At last they were quiet.

Susan had been so still that her legs and arms were

stiff. She shivered even though the blanket was wrapped tightly around her and Lame One was warm against her back.

There was no sound in the house now but deep breathing and the snoring of Grandmother. Susan quietly unrolled from the blanket. There must be no creaking on the floor or barking from Lame One. She would walk through the woods in the moccasins Father had made for her. They were like the foot of a rabbit. She quickly slipped them over her feet, then pulled on her blue sweater and gray skirt. She lifted Lame One in her arms and walked out the door.

The green-white light of the moon silenced the forest. The aspen leaves that always shimmered hung like black stones. The tall pines were dark, with every needle pressed against the sky.

Susan dropped Lame One onto the ground and began walking along a forest path. She had never seen shadows so large and so black. Hers looked like a giant with long, stiff arms. Lame One's shadow was a fox, with sharp, pointed ears.

Susan tried not to be afraid. She would soon meet Jim, and Lame One hobbled close beside her. She began to think of Uncle John and his stories about the Chippewa. They had lived in this forest many years before white men came to America. Some of the old people talked of ancestor spirits. Tonight it was easy for Susan to imagine them in the woods.

Uncle John had once told of a time when white men had ordered the Chippewa to leave Wisconsin and move far away to the West. Benjamin Armstrong, the brave adopted son of Chief Buffalo, had said no. He and his father went by birchbark canoe across the Great Lakes to Buffalo, New York. When they got there they had no money and soldiers had tried to send them home. But they sold Chippewa beads and bracelets and sat while curious people took their pictures. In this way they made enough money to buy railroad tickets to Washington, D.C. They went to see Millard Fillmore, the thirteenth President of the United States. Because Mr. Armstrong and Chief Buffalo were brave and honest, President Fillmore said that the Chippewa should never be moved from the state of Wisconsin.

Susan knew every word of the story. It was her favorite. It was the one Uncle John liked to tell best. When she thought of the courage of Chief Buffalo and his love for the land where she lived, it seemed wrong to move away from it.

A shadow flashed over Susan and she jumped. From the dark trees it whirred toward her, swooping close to her head. Lame One barked and tried to jump upward on his two back legs. There was a wavering cry, Hooooooo-hoo! Hooooooo-hoo.

A little screech owl! Susan looked up into the tree

and laughed. Its big, sad eyes stared down at her as though watching each toss of her head.

Such a tall, straight tree, Susan thought, looking up again at the hooting owl. Could it be . . . ?

She searched the ground at the foot of the trunk. There were the low, fat pines that couldn't grow upward. There was the crooked pine that bent beneath an outstretched branch of the tall pine. It was familiar and yet strange and different in the moonlight.

This must be the Tallest Pine! But where was Jim? Susan called his name. Her voice sounded hollow. It echoed through the woods and grew higher and higher until it joined the cry of the screech owl.

There was no answer. Only the Hooooo-hoo of the owl above her head.

Lame One lay panting on the thick brown pine needles. Susan sat beside him and rubbed his head. Jim had not come to the Tallest Pine. He had not built a fire or spread his blanket over the pine needles. A great hurt came to her throat and the need for tears to her eyes. But Susan swallowed hard and lifted Lame One in her arms. They must hurry home before anyone noticed her empty blanket roll on the floor. Now she knew that Jim wasn't coming home and that tomorrow she was going to Chicago.

7

LITTLE FLOWER, Little Flower."

Susan stirred sleepily inside her warm blanket roll. It was Mother's voice calling her. Susan opened her eyes. Out-of-doors it was still dark. Only the beginning of morning had come with the chirping of one small bird. Was it another day of harvest?

The lantern burned on the table and Grandmother stood with a sober face by the stove, fanning the chips of wood into a flame. Father entered the door, carrying a bucket of water from the well.

"There is time for dressing and eating," he said, "but we must not be late for the train."

The train. Today they were leaving and going to

Chicago. A bitter sickness spread inside her stomach and Susan knew she could not eat one bite of the food Grandmother was preparing. She wanted to cry aloud and shout an angry protest. But there was no one to take her side — not even Grandmother or Uncle John. She reached for Lame One, who slept beside her, and held him close.

"You must forgive me, Lame One," Susan whispered in his ear. "I do not want to go away from you. Stay with Grandmother. Someday I will come home."

Tears filled Susan's eyes. She brushed them away and crawled from the warmness of the blanket. She would not cry before Mother and Father and tall, courageous Grandmother. Mother handed her the new dress and she quickly slipped it on. Yesterday she had ached to wear it. This morning the cloth felt stiff and crinkly. The yellow daisies were not bright and cheerful in the lamp light.

She pushed her bare feet into the shining black shoes. Her toes could not move! She wondered if the feeling was like that of a bear with its paws in a trap. She must roll her moccasins inside her blanket and take them to Chicago. When her feet could no longer walk in the shoes, she would put on the moccasins.

Grandmother placed hot fried bread and corn cooked with turnips on the table. Susan could not eat. A great lump came to her throat each time she tried to swallow. Lame One sniffed at her feet and she pressed some of the bread into his mouth. If only she could take Lame One with her. But Father said dogs could not live in the city. Lame One must stay at home with Grandmother. She had never been away from the little dog. What would he do without her?

A car drove from the highway and stopped in front of the door. It was Uncle John! Susan had forgotten about Uncle John and the talk of his borrowing a car from Striking Thunder to take them to the train.

Susan put on the soft blue coat and squeezed it around her. She smoothed her black hair over the collar. In the new shoes, the new dress, and the new coat only her hair felt real — as though it were the only thing that honestly belonged to her.

Uncle John motioned for Susan to sit in front with him. She nodded, then turned to say good-bye to Grandmother and Lame One. Grandmother came to the door, standing tall and straight, as she always did for solemn occasions.

"Remember, Little Flower, have courage and be proud that you are a Chippewa," she said.

Susan looked at Grandmother's strong face with the wrinkles about her eyes and mouth that could smile or be sad, as they were now. She knew that she would try to obey her.

Susan called Lame One, but he didn't come. Perhaps he had gone to play with the other dogs of the reservation.

Uncle John laughed, "The dog is here, in the seat beside me!"

Father lifted the small dog from the car and handed him to Grandmother.

"Now come," he motioned to Mother and Susan. "We must leave at once."

Susan held her blanket roll with the moccasins inside tightly against her. If only she could roll Lame One inside it too. She touched the dog quickly on the head and ran to the car.

She could not look back as the car drove from the house. This time she could not hide the tears in her eyes. The road in front of them and the tall rows of pine trees on either side were blurs of green and brown that went on and on.

Was Grandmother still standing in the doorway? she wondered. Was Lame One hobbling down the road trying to reach her?

At last the car stopped before the railway station. "We will put our bags by the tracks and wait for the train here," Father told Susan and Mother as he walked from the car, placing their two new suitcases and a large blanket roll on the platform. Father had traveled on the train before. He called it an "Iron Horse." For Mother and Susan, this was their first trip.

"Susan," Uncle John looked at her with concern and reached into his pocket, "I made something at my college which I want you to take to Chicago."

He opened a small box. Inside Susan saw a silver ring. She bent closer. The design on top was the head of a lion.

Uncle John slipped it onto her fourth finger. It was smooth and shiny. Susan looked at it carefully. The design honored the totem of her family — the lion totem.

"You are going to live in a white man's world, Little Flower," Uncle John spoke slowly, as though wanting her to remember each word. "Be brave enough to be someone in that world. Learn as much as you can. Then come back and help your tribe. The ring will help you to remember."

People began walking from the station and placing their bags near Father's. A warning light blinked red near the railroad crossing. A large bell clanged loudly beside it. The train was coming. Its giant engine slowed to a stop in front of them. It hissed with steam and dripped with oil and muddy water.

A man in a black uniform motioned for them to come to a small metal box where they stepped onto the stairs that led into the train.

"Turn left to Chicago," he shouted.

Father led the way, carrying their bags. At the far end of the car two benches faced each other. Susan and Mother stopped and Father swung their suitcases onto a rack above their heads. Susan sat near the window on one bench and Mother on the other. Father took his place beside Mother. Other passengers crowded into the car and threw their baggage on the little rack.

Susan sat without moving, clutching the blanket roll in front of her. She touched the ring. The lion's head felt firm and strong. But the blue coat was hot and prickly. Susan was afraid to stand and take it off. Mother pulled her fringed shawl about her shoulders and tied her silk headscarf tightly under her chin. Only Father removed his new hat and placed it in his lap.

The train began to move, slowly at first, and then with more and more speed. When Susan looked out the window she tried to find Uncle John, but he had disappeared. She had forgotten to tell him good-bye. She had not even thanked him for the ring.

Susan could not recognize the trees or the roads which sped by them. The forests were different. The highways were strange. The little houses were new. She had never seen any of them before.

An old man came down the aisle pushing a cart. Without moving her head Susan could see apples, candy bars, bottles of Coke, and sandwiches wrapped in transparent paper. Susan was hungry now, but she knew Father would not buy this food. The man stopped beside them.

"Speaka English?" he asked and then waited.

Father said nothing and looked straight ahead. Susan's face flushed. She did not want the man to think they could not speak English. She wondered why he had asked.

The man moved on. He stopped at the next row of seats where people laughed and bought many drinks and candy bars.

The old man leaned over his cart.

"The Indians back there don't speak English. I don't know what they'll do when they get to Chicago."

"Maybe they'll hunt bears at Lincoln Park Zoo," a woman with a high voice giggled.

Father spoke quietly in the language of the Chippewa. "They must think we do not live in America."

Susan saw a thin smile about his mouth and knew he thought this was a joke. Susan wanted to smile with him, but she could not think it funny. Father could speak English and he would not hunt bears in a city.

The scenery began to change. The towns drew closer and closer together. The green forests were a blur in the distance. Now there were only clumps of trees along the river or bunches of them clustered around the little towns. Soon there were fewer trees and only rows of houses and clumps of buildings with great signs on them that had no meaning to Susan.

Susan's neck grew stiff, but she could not turn her eyes from the window. She had to look each minute or she would miss a changing scene. Now there were no houses — only tall buildings, flat buildings, and wide buildings piled together like the boxes in the storeroom of the Lac du Flambeau grocery. How did people walk between them?

She began to think how she would tell Grandmother and Mary and Louise about the scrambled buildings. But when would she see them again? The sickness she felt earlier in the morning swept over her. A pain throbbed against her heart. Her feet ached and the new coat scratched her neck and her wrists.

Suddenly the bright sun that shone through their window disappeared. It was dark. The train seemed to be traveling into one of the buildings. Susan closed her eyes in terror. The motion of the train slowed down. Their car creaked and jerked and then stopped. Susan opened her eyes.

"We are in Chicago," Father announced quietly.

People moved from their seats and reached above their heads for their baggage. Susan wondered if she could stand. She hadn't moved her legs since they got on the train.

Father's hand shook as he pulled a sheet of paper from his pocket. Susan knew that it was a list of instructions from the Bureau of Indian Affairs in Chicago. It told what they should do when they got inside the railroad station and how they should get a car called a taxi to take them to the bureau office.

When Susan stood, her feet felt like they had been pressed into a tiny box and would soon explode. The shoes were like bear traps. Susan wondered if clanging metal were hanging on each shoe as she tried to lift her feet. Outside the train, people raced along as though a swarm of bees were chasing them. Father moved aside to let them pass and then walked inside the station. She had never seen a room so large or a ceiling so high. Round pillars rose from the floor to the ceiling as high as the Tallest Pine. People swarmed around them like ants over an upturned hill.

She stared at all the people around her, especially those with black skins. Susan knew they were Negroes, but she had never seen one before. She was startled when Mother touched her shoulder and said in Chippewa, "Indians do not stare, Little Flower."

Father pointed to a sign which read "taxi." A long arrow told them that they should go down a flight of stairs. Father picked up the bags and started toward them. At the top he stopped abruptly and looked over the side. Mother and Susan joined him. The stairs were rolling down and down without stopping.

"It is a waterfall!" Susan cried. How did the people move down them and get off at the bottom? Susan watched a mother and a little boy step over the side and grab the moving rail. They were not afraid. They laughed and chatted with each other.

Father moved one foot forward to get on.

"No!" Mother shouted. She held her blanket roll against her stomach and stood motionless. "I will not go down the waterfall!"

Susan knew that Mother, who was usually afraid to speak in public, meant what she said.

A Negro woman walked toward them. "There's some steps over yonder," she said, and smiled. "You can walk down those."

Father thanked her and they walked to a stairway with solid steps that did not move. Mother started down them, holding carefully to a wooden rail along the side.

When they walked outside the station, they saw rows of yellow taxis lining the street like a string of bright beads. The driver of one of them opened his door and the Bearskins stepped inside.

Father read aloud from the paper, "We want to go to the Relocation Office of the Bureau of Indian Affairs on Jackson Boulevard."

The driver nodded and whizzed into lines of moving cars. He reminded Susan of Jim, poling their canoe through the wild rice grass in the lake at home. Jim would be a good driver of a taxi. She wished he were with them now. Their car came to a bridge with a river running under it. There were no trees or grass along the sides — only tall buildings packed together with their basements in the water.

"This is a city river," Susan whispered to Mother.

The taxi scraped over the bridge like a canoe rubbing its floor against a sand bar.

Several buildings from the bridge, the taxi stopped. A little box, ticking in front of them, told Father how much he must pay. It was more than a dollar! Susan couldn't believe that one short car trip could cost so much.

"You take the elevator to the eleventh floor," the taxi driver called and drove away.

Susan had read about an elevator. She wondered if Mother would ride in it. But Mother was tired and hot and hadn't heard what the man said. She followed Father and Susan into the little box where other people stood together waiting for them. A man closed all the people inside with a sliding door. He pressed a button and the box shot up. Susan thought her stomach was being pushed into her head. Mother grabbed Father's arm and closed her eyes.

In a moment the elevator stopped. The doors slid

open, and the Bearskins walked into the office of the Bureau of Indian Affairs.

There were Indians in the office! Some of them were seated on a green bench against the wall. Others stood behind little desks. Susan sat on a bench and unbuttoned the blue coat. Then she reached inside the blanket roll and pulled out the moccasins. She pushed the black bear traps off her feet and slid into the soft, cool moccasins. Before anyone noticed, she stuffed the new shoes inside the blanket.

8

Susan stretched her feet back and forth inside the softness of her moccasins. She noticed the stiff toes of the new black shoes poking through her blanket. They were as hard as the city streets, she thought.

A white woman with large black-rimmed glasses motioned for Father to come to her desk. Susan watched her push papers in front of him and give him a pen. She talked rapidly, moving her hands and fingers in front of her as though directing her own speech.

"Describe your son," she said to Father. "What is his height? What is his weight?"

Susan was surprised. Wasn't it more important that

Jim was the fastest runner of Lac du Flambeau, and that he could swim through Rice Lake until his head moved more swiftly than the boats with motors?

Father and the white woman lowered their voices. She saw Father write on the papers. Then the white woman picked them up with her long fingers and slipped them into a rolling drawer.

"We will go now." She raised her voice and nodded to Mother, Susan, and Father in rapid succession. Then she snapped the lock on her leather bag and slung its long handle over her shoulder.

"Susan — Mrs. Bearskin — welcome to Chicago." Her wide smile was generous. Susan liked her, but she wondered about a woman who moved as quickly as the chipmunk and who talked with a running tongue.

The Indian Bureau woman hurried the family into the elevator box again. Mother gripped Father's arm and closed her eyes for the entire trip. Susan liked dropping down better than pushing up. It reminded her of falling into Rice Lake from the spreading branch of the white birch.

The white lady didn't stop talking. She stood near the elevator man, moving her lips and waving her hands.

"I will call her Running Tongue," Susan decided, and she had to put her hand over her mouth to hide the laughter which she couldn't stop.

Outside the building Miss Running Tongue waved

to a yellow taxi. It stopped beside them and she directed Susan, Mother, and Father to the back seat. She pulled a little chair from the floor and turned it around to face them.

"This way I can tell you about everything as we ride along." She interrupted herself long enough to hand the taxi driver a slip of paper with the address of the Bearskin home printed on it.

She unsnapped her bulging leather bag and pulled out a box which she handed to Father.

"Mr. Bearskin," she said soberly, as though the box might contain a secret treasure. "Inside this box is a small alarm clock. The city is different from the reservation. Here, everything is done at an exact time. You must report at an exact time for your grocery store job each day. Susan must leave at an exact time for her school every day. Mrs. Bearskin will want to know the exact time you are coming home — so she can have your meals ready, exactly on time."

Susan couldn't stop looking at Running Tongue's mouth. She seemed to take a bite from the air each time she said "exact."

"We are going to the north side of Chicago," her words rushed on, and her head bobbed back and forth from the side to the back windows. "You will live on Clark Street. The apartments are low rent and not the best, but someday, Mr. Bearskin, if you save your money and work hard, you can move to a better neighborhood . . . . perhaps even buy a home of your own."

Indians do not save money, Susan wanted to shout the words but her lips did not move. We buy food and clothes with it!

Didn't Running Tongue know that Indian families did not buy land and houses? The tribe owned the houses, and the land was only used and shared. No one owned it!

Running Tongue abruptly stopped her speech and looked out the window. She bent toward the taxi driver.

"Turn left so we can drive past Susan's school."

"My school!" This time Susan's words *could* be heard.

She had never thought about her city school. She was frightened as they approached it. She would not have one friend. The teacher would be new. How would she know where to go and what to do?

She pressed her face against the car window and wondered how a school could fit between the packed apartments and squeezed-in stores that lined the streets.

"It's only five blocks from your apartment, Susan. You can walk, and you will start tomorrow morning *exactly* at nine o'clock. Your Mother can take you." Running Tongue drummed her fingers impatiently on her leather bag as the taxi stopped for a red light.

Mother looked up with alarm.

"Don't be frightened, Mrs. Bearskin," Running Tongue said, and swept her hand through the air as though erasing all concern. "The principal welcomes parents. . . . There will be a small cost for Susan's books. . . . She can take a lunch with her. . . . I have printed all this information on a paper for you."

She handed the paper to Father.

"Here we are, here we are at last," Running Tongue said, and sighed as though she might relax. She even took off her black-rimmed glasses and folded them in her lap. The taxi driver slowed down as they approached a thick, red brick building. Susan gasped. The building started at one end of the block and went on and on to the next street. Long rows of high, thin windows cut into the walls and heavy wire criss-crossed over some of them. They were like the windows of the jail in Manitoish near the building where Jim was taken the night before he ran away!

Running Tongue sensed Susan's alarm.

"The wire on the lower windows," she said in a matter-of-fact voice, "is to keep children from breaking them with rocks. . . . There are one thousand youngsters in the school now. It's hard to have adequate playground supervision for so many. . . . But don't let it worry you, Susan. . . . The boys are the window breakers. . . . The girls play over there." She pointed to a wide cement space at the back of the school with a high board fence behind it.

What would the girls play on hard cement? Susan thought of the school at Lac du Flambeau. It would fit into one small corner of this giant building. At home the playground was green with grass.

"Grass doesn't grow in the city," Susan remarked quietly. "The earth is cement. It must be needed to hold up all the buildings."

The taxi turned a corner onto Clark Street.

"Your street!" Running Tongue announced, whisking her glasses into place.

The taxi stopped before a gray stone building. Susan noticed a little square of dirt in front of the door and two dirty children scratching in it with sticks.

Running Tongue jumped from the car. Mother, Susan, and Father grabbed their bags and blanket rolls and hurried to keep up with her. She opened the front door of the building and pressed her finger on a little brass button. A buzzing sound shook the knob and she pushed the door open.

Running Tongue explained, "This is your button. . . . The building manager will tell you how to use it and he will give you keys."

She walked ahead of them up a narrow row of stairs to a hallway, and then up more stairs. Susan grabbed the fullness of Mother's skirt. She couldn't see.

Like the hole of a spider, Susan thought, as the light from the doorway grew dimmer.

At the top of the second stairway, Running Tongue stopped before a door. She twisted a key into a small hole and the door opened. It was dark. She switched on a light.

"Now don't be alarmed by the dark," Running Tongue said, and looked about quickly and pushed her glasses back and forth as though trying to get a better view. "There are windows, but the building next door is so close, the sun just can't shine through. . . ."

The room was small. A bulging green sofa crouched like a fat bullfrog at one end of the room. At the other end was a heavy mud-brown chair. Wire springs poked through the dirty covers.

Running Tongue pushed one of the springs into the cloth. "One of these days, Mrs. Bearskin, you'll want to buy some nice, fresh cloth and put new covers on this old furniture. . . . Now come along. . . . Here is the kitchen with a gas stove. . . . Now watch me. Light a match, turn the knob, and you have a flame."

"It is magic," Susan whispered to Mother.

The kitchen was dark, too, until Father opened a back door and sunshine poured in. Susan walked out the door onto a small back porch. She leaned over the side rail. Below her, little orange and red flags whipped around in the wind over the top of a long sign which spelled USED CAR LOT. The letters were formed with light bulbs! The cars below were packed together side by side like minnows on the shallow sand bar of Rice Lake.

Susan searched for trees and green grass. As far as she could see from the little porch, the earth was covered with streets and buildings.

Running Tongue called from the kitchen. "I wouldn't go down those zig-zag back stairs, Susan. . . . The owner of the lot doesn't like children running about and scratching his cars. . . . You'll get your exercise walking to and from school. Maybe some Saturday, your mother can take you on a bus to Lincoln Park."

Susan nodded wearily. She could no longer remember all the things she was not supposed to do. She decided to stay on the porch. It was better than the dark house without daylight.

Running Tongue came to the back door and pointed to a large clock on the wall of a building across the street. She threw her hands above her head.

"Mercy, how time flies. . . . I must fly myself. . . . Here is my phone number, Mr. Bearskin. Call if you need help. . . . The telephone is downstairs in the hallway." She opened her purse and shook it up and down until she found a yellow paper which she gave to Father. "Follow these directions. You'll have no trouble at all. . . . I know you'll love Chicago. . . . I've lived here all my life. . . . There isn't a better city in the world!"

She opened the door quickly and called back to them as she went down the stairs, "You're going to get along fine. . . . Don't forget to set your alarm to-night. . . . Good-bye!"

Father closed the door and walked back to the porch. Susan thought she saw a small smile on his face.

"I have given the lady a name," Susan said, "I call her Running Tongue."

Father's smile became a laugh. He leaned against the porch rail and bent forward laughing. Mother and Susan joined him.

"She is a good woman who is helping us," Father said, as he wiped his eyes with the back of his hand. "But her tongue runs faster than Jim's feet."

Jim!

Mother, Susan, and Father were silent.

All of them had hoped to find Jim in Chicago. If he were with them now, Susan thought, he could help her find the school tomorrow. He could go with Mother to buy some food. He could listen with Father for the ringing alarm clock. He would not be afraid of the crowded sidewalks with the racing people or the crowded streets with the racing cars.

"I will find Jim, if I have to walk up and down every street in Chicago," Susan announced firmly.

Father patted her hand. Mother tried to smile in spite of the tears that blurred her eyes.

"He will go home to Grandmother," she said.

Mother opened one of her baskets and took out some dried fruit cakes and cold fried bread.

"Tonight, we will eat here in this house." Mother spread a red cloth over the scratched kitchen table. "I have seen enough of the rushing and the people."

Father agreed. He joined Susan on the little porch and they both looked into the sky. A red ball of sun glowed behind the used car sign, outlining the edges of it with gold.

"It is the same sun that shines on our forest," Father said with a sigh, "but it does not put the city to sleep. There are lights going on like stars." He swept his arm over the car lot below. The light bulbs that spelled Used Car Lot flashed on. They blinked like the eyes of a hundred owls.

Susan felt strangeness and fear of the city surround her. She reached for Father's hand.

"There is no night here for sleeping," she said.

"Don't forget, Susan," Father said with a chuckle, "there is night all the time in our living room."

9

THE MORNING SUNLIGHT streaked through the dusty window into the Bearskin kitchen. Susan blinked her eyes and lifted her head from the soft folds of her Indian blanket. Why was she on the floor of this faded green room? What was Father doing at the strange table holding a little clock? Why did Mother light matches over a white, square stove?

She was in Chicago! Tiny particles of dust swirled before her eyes. She wondered if she was going to be sick.

Today she must go to the brick school that stretched from one street to another. There would be more children than the needles on a pine tree, and she would not know one of them.

Father smiled at her and shook the little clock.

"The clock speaks to us, Little Flower," he said. "It tells us that we have one more hour before the beginning of your school."

Susan jumped up. She reached for the new dress that hung from a nail near the door and began to shake the wrinkles from it. She winced and slid her bare feet into the heavy school shoes.

Who would go to school with her?

Mother was bewildered by the white stove.

"Running Tongue made the flame leap out with a match," Mother said, and shook her head. "How can there be a fire when there is no burning wood?"

Father looked for directions in the yellow sheets of paper. There were none. He searched behind the stove and opened the door in the front. There was no place for fuel.

"We will eat cold fried bread from last night," Mother said finally. She handed a piece to Susan and Father. They drank water that ran from the pipe on the wall.

Susan could not swallow the bread, even though her stomach ached with hunger.

The clock now said forty-five minutes until the school would start!

Father slowly drank a cup of the water and then stood and reached for his new wide-brimmed hat.

"I will go to the school with Susan before my job

must start at the grocery store." His calm, dark eyes watched Mother, who shook the cold coffeepot and then put it on the table. She threw her Indian blanket over the stove and entirely covered it.

"Maybe the blanket will warm it up," Father laughed. "Tonight I will bring food from this grocery store. If Running Tongue can make a fire, we can make a fire."

A lump disappeared from Susan's throat and she swallowed her fried bread. If Father went to the school with her it would not be so frightening.

"I will stay in this room until you come home tonight," Mother announced, standing with folded arms and frightened eyes beside the stove.

"You will have the clock for noise," Father said, and smiled at her. "It will tell you *exactly* when we come home."

Mother tried to laugh, but there was no happiness on her face.

Susan wanted to stay in the room with her, but Father was already hurrying down the long dark stairway. Susan followed. When they opened the front door, they saw men and women walking rapidly along the sidewalk. None of them spoke or turned their heads.

With such stiff heads and straight walking, they would be good in the Deer Dance, Susan thought and smiled to herself.

A tall woman in front of them yanked a silver chain that was tied to the neck of a fat dog. The dog sniffed and tried to scratch in the little dirt yard. It growled at Susan. She was glad Lame One had not come to the city. He would not like a chain pulling at his neck.

Father reached for Susan's hand. "You must look at all the stores along the street so you can find your way home tonight alone."

Alone! The lump tightened in Susan's throat again and she choked. She felt in her pocket for the slip of paper that had the address of their building.

At home in the forest, Susan could remember new paths. Each tree was different and the sun told the time and direction. In the city, the buildings covered the sun.

Susan began to watch. Next to their apartment house was a shop with stiff white shirts hanging in the window. On the corner across from them, a door swung back and forth when people banged against it. Cars rushed along their street with the angry screech of crows.

They turned off Clark and walked on Elm Street. Rows of gray stone buildings hovered against the sidewalk, scarcely allowing room for the dirty children that played in front of them.

At the end of the block, Susan saw the school.

A shrill bell rang. Hundreds of boys and girls ran

from every direction and melted into long, thin lines which streamed into the doors.

"We will go to the biggest door in the middle," Father said as he took her hand in his. It was cold but firm. As long as Father was with her she would not be afraid. They walked through the open door. Inside, they looked up and down the long corridors. No sign or direction on the sheet of paper told them which way to go.

A tall white woman with red hair walked toward them. She spoke crisply, barely moving her thin lips. "If you are new here and want to enroll, walk to your left to the principal's office." She left them.

Father tightened his grip on Susan's hand. Inside the room marked Principal there were other boys and girls with their mothers and fathers, waiting in a line to see a tall, thin man behind a desk. Susan thought of a pumpkin when she saw the smoothness of his bald head.

MR. MALONEY, PRINCIPAL, a sign on his desk read.

Susan glanced quickly at the other boys and girls in the line. Many of them did not have white skin. But they were not Indians. She listened to the principal.

"Where were you born?" he asked, looking into one of their faces.

"Puerto Rico," the boy answered.

Susan had never heard of such a place. Tonight she

would look in the book of maps Uncle John had given her and find it. She looked shyly about the room to see if there might be others from this strange country.

At the far end of the room was a tall black-haired boy bending over a desk. His back was toward her. He wore new blue jeans and a plaid shirt like Jim's. He looked like Jim. It was Jim! He had come to Chicago to go to school. Forgetting everyone else in the room, Susan grabbed Father's hand and started toward him.

"Jim!" she shouted.

The children and their parents turned around to look at her. The black-haired boy jerked his head about. His face was round. His eyes were small and sullen. It was not Jim.

Susan was confused. Her face felt hot and flushed. She wanted to run from the room and hide.

Mr. Maloney stood behind his desk. A row of wrinkles frowned at her over the top of his bald head.

"Young lady," he spoke crisply, like the red-haired lady in the hall. "We do not shout in here. This is a schoolroom, not a playground."

He sat down and began talking to the next family in the line.

Father whispered to Susan in Chippewa. "In the back the boy does look like Jim. In the front, our Jim looks better."

Susan agreed.

When it was Susan's turn to stand before the principal, she could not look at him. She was too ashamed. He rustled the papers which Father gave him from the reservation school.

"Sorry to be in such a hurry," he said, making notes in a big book. "But this school is located in a changing neighborhood. Children go in and out of here every week. You Indian people move around a lot, too."

A boy behind Susan whispered loudly, "Did you hear that, she's one of those wild Indians! She better not be in my room."

The principal had not heard. Susan did not dare turn around. Her head began to ache. She tried to remember Grandmother's words. "Close your eyes and your ears to the white man when he speaks with cruelty or lies. Look through him as though he were not there."

Susan did not turn her head, but she could not forget the words of the loud whisper.

Mr. Maloney leafed again through the papers, the skin on his bald head folding into wrinkles.

This time he talked directly to Susan. "You haven't been in school enough to go to the seventh grade where you belong," he said. "I'll have to put you in grade four."

Susan didn't mind. She would go to any grade just to get out of this room. She tried not to look, but she couldn't help seeing the boy who had whispered. He was holding a stack of books and looked as though he might be helping Mr. Maloney. His yellow hair was a stubble of short-cut straw, and his round, fat face had two punched-in blueberries for eyes. They narrowed to thin slits when Susan looked into them.

"You may go now, Mr. Bearskin," Mr. Maloney waved Father off in the opposite direction. "Thank you for coming."

Oh, no! Susan cried inside, but her face did not change expression. I want to go with Father! Without saying a word, however, she followed a small boy down the hall to a room marked, Grade 4, Miss Turner.

The boy knocked, and the door was opened by the red-haired lady with the small prim mouth.

"Are you sure she belongs in here?" Miss Turner's small mouth barely moved, but her words were clear and firm.

The boy handed her some papers from Mr. Maloney.

Susan walked inside. She looked at rows of staring faces. They belonged to little children! These boys and girls were no bigger than cousin Mary on the reservation, who would soon be only nine years old.

Miss Turner moved a big chair to the back of the room.

"Sit here, Susan," she said quickly. "You are too big for the desks." The chair was stiff and black, with high legs that stood above the little desks around it. It creaked when Susan sat down.

The staring children began to laugh.

"Quiet!" Miss Turner's small mouth had a large voice behind it.

Susan was thankful that the children were obedient. The room became as still as Rice Lake under a mist. Miss Turner began writing on the board. Everyone watched and listened. She talked about a river called the Mississippi that ran down the center of the United States. Susan had never heard of this great river. She would try to find it tonight in Uncle John's book when she looked for Puerto Rico. She forgot for a moment that her long legs felt as awkward as logs in a forest path in this room of little people.

A loud, jarring buzz interrupted.

"Recess time," Miss Turner announced.

Miss Turner stood on her toes and looked toward the back of the room. "Susan," she said, "follow the class to the playground. When the bell rings, line up at the same door where you go out."

The little staring faces turned in her direction.

Susan pulled her legs under the chair and slid down in her seat, trying to make herself as small as possible. If only Miss Turner hadn't called everyone's attention to her again.

"Take your place in the line, Susan," Miss Turner's voice was softer and not so crisp.

Susan walked toward the end of the line. She passed Miss Turner. She was almost as tall as her teacher! The class began marching through the door and down the long hall.

A little fat boy in front of Susan turned around and asked bluntly, "Are you an Indian?"

All the staring faces watched for her answer. Susan didn't know why she hesitated. The determined eyes of the fat boy demanded an answer.

"Yes," Susan said finally.

"Do you come from India?" a girl beside the fat boy wanted to know.

Susan couldn't speak. She shook her head.

The fat boy spoke again.

"Are all Indians as big as you?"

Susan was thankful she did not have to answer. They had reached the school door and everyone raced outside. But the little staring faces did not leave her. The boys formed a ring around her and began to whoop and shriek and pound each other over the heads. A big boy with straw-yellow hair joined them. He was the same boy who had whispered about her in the principal's office.

The big boy yelled, "Let's tie her to a stake. Let's burn her!" Susan was terrified. What should she do?

She wanted to run from the school. She wanted to be with Mother. How could she get through the crowds of children? They were on every side of her.

Laughing girls jumped over a swinging rope. Shouting boys bounced a ball against the side of the great school building. Susan clasped her hands together and pressed Uncle John's ring. She felt the strong, brave head of the lion. Uncle John said it would be hard to live in a white man's world.

The bell rang! The yelling boys ran for their lines. Susan was pale and weak. Her class of little staring faces lined up behind her and she led them into the school building. She welcomed the safety of the quiet classroom. She wanted to listen to Miss Turner. If only the dreaded bell would never ring.

Miss Turner was pulling a large map of the world from a roller on the wall when the buzzing bell sounded again. She snapped it back into the roller and announced, "Time for lunch!"

Lunch! Susan and Mother had forgotten about Running Tongue's words on lunch. Susan had none. She followed the little children to a basement room with tables and benches. Everyone had sacks with food inside them.

Susan's stomach pinched with hunger. She looked at a hole in the ceiling where there was no one to stare back at her. She was startled when a lady with a face from Puerto Rico stopped in front of her. She handed Susan a glass of milk and a large, sugar dough-nut.

"Thank you," Susan managed to say.

The milk was thick with cream. The sweetness of the doughnut spread through her stomach like Grandmother's berry cakes always did.

After lunch there were more classes. At last, the final bell rang. It clanged louder than the others. Susan was glad and terrified that the school day was ending. What if she could not remember the streets or the buildings near their home?

She reached in her pocket and felt the crumpled piece of paper with their address on it. The words of Running Tongue raced through her mind. "Ask a policeman if you ever get lost. Always remember the address of your building."

Children spilled from the school, flowing in all directions like rivulets from a swollen stream at flood time. Susan began looking for the shop with the white shirts and the store with the swinging door. She hoped the boy, whom she had named Straw Hair, lived in another direction. She was afraid to look at the children around her.

If she could only find Jim. He was never afraid. He must be someplace in Chicago. Tomorrow she would look for him. She felt for the crumpled paper in her pocket again. It was there. But the number and the street name didn't help. She wouldn't ask anyone for help. Susan turned down Clark Street. There were no white shirts in any of the windows. Susan was terrified. Then she saw the patch of dirty yard. It was in front of her building.

She raced to the front door and ran up the dark stairway. The dusty air made her cough. She pressed the little button that was a doorbell and frantically called, "Mother."

"Susan!" She could hear Mother's eager reply on the other side.

When the door opened, she ran into Mother's arms and sobbed. The stiff face that she had worn all day dissolved in tears.

Mother stroked her hair. "It is harder to see the city, Little Flower, than to hide as I have today." They walked to the boxlike porch where they sat on Indian blankets that Mother spread on the floor.

The doorbell rang again. It was Father. His new clothes were streaked with dirt. His shoulders bent with tiredness. But he carried sacks of food in both arms.

"I did not ask about the stove," he said, putting the sacks on the kitchen table. Mother and Susan understood. "But we can eat all of this food without cooking it."

10

Susan ate a hard cracker and drank a glass of cold milk for breakfast. The taste was like dust blown from the path of the pine forest at home. She thought of Grandmother and the wood-burning stove in their shack, where the delicious smell of the cooking food was as good as the taste of it later.

She must ask Father for twenty cents to buy hot soup at school today.

The school!

It was a snarling fox in her mind. It was frightening and unpredictable. At home she was *Little* Flower. At school she was an awkward giant. At Lac du Flambeau, all the Chippewa boys and girls were her friends. At the city school, Straw Hair and his friends were her enemies on the first day. How could she tell Mother and Father of this great trouble? They were already filled with their own worries.

"White men in the city follow the clock," Father protested. "They are punished if they disobey it."

Mother stood by the unused stove, wiping the top of it with a cloth. She pushed the cold coffeepot away from the fireless burner.

"If a letter comes from Jim," she asked, "will it be brought to this house?"

Father frowned.

"I thought of Jim all of yesterday," he said. "He will camp in the forest for a week and then go home to Grandmother. We must not worry about him."

Susan knew better. Jim was not in the forest. He was someplace in this crowded, noisy city. He would have nothing left of Uncle John's five dollars. How would he pay for a place to sleep? What would he eat? She must start looking for him today.

The ticking clock moved closer to the number which told Susan and Father that it was time to go. Mother watched it too and sadness spread over her face. Susan knew that the day would be lonely for Mother until the sun moved to the west and she came home from the school.

Today she and Father walked in silence to the end of Clark Street. They stopped for a moment before she turned at the street called Elm.

"Chicago is a place of many paths, Little Flower." Father spoke in the language of the Chippewa. "I think a Chippewa can learn to use them as well as the white man."

He turned quickly and walked away.

Susan heard the shouting noises from the school playground.

"It is like hawks screaming over dead fish," she thought, wishing she could escape from it.

She hesitated when she reached the school ground. Then she decided to push her way to the door and be first in line when the bell rang. Maybe she wouldn't be noticed. She squeezed around two tall girls who were jumping rope.

"They are my size!" Susan realized, and for a moment she wanted to sing their songs and run through their swinging rope.

"Hi!" a loud voice yelled in front of her, "here comes the Indian!"

It was Straw Hair. His face was red and his hair poked above his head like porcupine quills.

Susan's heart pounded and her legs trembled. But she looked straight ahead as though he were not there.

Straw Hair pranced around her in an Indian dance, shouting and jerking his head up and down. A row of little boys followed behind him.

Susan wanted to hide her face in her hands and

race through the crowds of children, running until she came to the green forest of the reservation. But her face remained motionless. Inside, her heart beat wildly and her hands grew hot and then cold. She clenched them together so tightly that Uncle John's ring pinched her finger. The bell rang and Straw Hair ran to his line.

Susan looked at the ring and the lion totem that Uncle John had carved so carefully on the top of it.

"Be proud that you are a Chippewa," Uncle John said when he gave it to her. A tear slipped from her eye and splashed onto the lion head. What did Uncle John want her to do in this playground?

Susan walked to her line with the little children. Today Miss Turner stood at the door. Everyone became silent immediately. Susan was relieved. No one could ask her a question. When they entered the classroom, she hurried to her big chair in the back row.

Miss Turner talked about people in strange countries who were different from most Americans. She wrote number problems on the board. Susan could understand them. She tried to do one in her head. Her answer was correct!

"Clang . . . Clang." The bell! Recess!

Susan held her hands over her ears. If only the bell would never ring and there would never be a recess.

Desperately, she began to wonder if there might be

a place on the school ground where she could hide. She remembered some trash containers near the school door with a little wall around them. Maybe she could squeeze behind the wall and no one would see her until the recess was over.

Susan walked with her class to the outside door. Then she moved slowly away from them toward the wall. She couldn't see Straw Hair. Perhaps his class hadn't come outside yet. She slid behind the wall and squeezed between the cans. She ducked her head just in time, for she heard Straw Hair shouting, "Come on, let's see if we can find the Indian."

Susan held her breath. She could see the boy's head on the other side of the wall. He had a red bandana tied around it. She could even see the letter *"E"* stamped in one corner.

"That's funny," Susan heard Straw Hair mutter, "the Indian towers above those little kids in her class."

Straw Hair moved back and forth on the other side of the fence. He would see her if he turned around. There was a long silence.

"Say," Straw Hair finally said to the smaller boys, whose heads were hidden by the wall, "did you read in the newspaper about that spook in Lincoln Park?"

"Yeah," another boy said with a laugh, "some guy's been fishing in the lagoon and cooking his meals at night. The police find the fish bones and the ashes from the fire every morning."

"It sounds like some dumb Indian," Straw Hair commented as he began moving away from the wall to another part of the school yard.

"That's what the newspaper said," the other boy answered eagerly. "Somebody thinks they saw him and that it was an Indian boy."

An Indian cooking fish in Lincoln Park! It was Jim! Susan knew it must be Jim. If he were living in this Lincoln Park, she must go there and find him.

Susan did not move from her hiding place until the bell rang. She forgot about Straw Hair. She could think only of Lincoln Park, where Jim was hiding. In the classroom there was a map of Chicago. She would ask Miss Turner if she could look at it. She would remember the names of all the streets that led to Lincoln Park. Tomorrow she would not go to school. She would go to this park and find Jim. Mother and Father would be filled with joy when she brought him home.

Susan walked to Miss Turner's desk when she entered the room.

"I would like to look at the Chicago map." Her request was a whisper.

Miss Turner's small mouth smiled slightly in one corner.

"Of course!" her crisp words carried to every part of the room. "You are new in the city. You should have a small map of your own."

She opened the drawer of her desk and pulled out a black book. When it was opened a large map of Chicago unfolded from the center. Miss Turner leafed through the pages pointing out lists of buses, trains — and *parks!*

"You may have this." She snapped the book shut and dismissed Susan promptly with a wave of her hand.

Susan clasped both hands around the book. It was just what she needed! If she carried the book with h . she could not get lost. She would read all the pages about Lincoln Park.

When the final school bell rang and her class marched to the open door, Susan ran across the playground. She heard Straw Hair's loud voice shouting behind her, but she could not hear his words.

She raced down the street, her shoes clopping on the hard cement like rain on the tin roof of their shack at home. Faces blurred past her. A red light blinked and then flashed green. She turned down Clark Street and saw the dirty gray building where Mother would be waiting. As she pulled open the front door, Susan noticed a curtain being yanked shut on a nearby window. A face drew back, then disappeared. It was the face of Straw Hair!

11

Susan ate the cold food from Father's grocery sack that evening, but it had no taste. Two thoughts pounded in her head. Did Straw Hair live beside the front door of her apartment? If he did, how could she escape his cruel threats? Would she find Jim in Lincoln Park tomorrow? She must!

After Mother took the grocery sacks from the table, Susan unfolded her map of Chicago on it and began to study the spider-web lines that were the streets. Father helped her find the place where they lived and she marked it with a large X. She wanted to tell Mother and Father where she was going.

She started to speak and then closed her mouth, swallowing the words. Father might not believe the story of Straw Hair. Mother would be frightened by the strange trip. She would say no.

"This time I will be a mule-head," Susan decided. "I will go to this Lincoln Park without telling anyone. I know it is Jim who fishes in the night."

She looked at the spider-web streets again. She must go down the line marked North Avenue. It didn't look far. She could walk. She would save the lunch money for Jim.

Under *Parks*, the book told about Lincoln Park. It was near Lake Michigan. Susan remembered! This was the big blue lake surrounded by rows of white buildings that appeared in a picture on the Relocation Office wall at Lac du Flambeau. The map book also told about buses and how to pay fifteen cents to get on one marked Lincoln Park. What if she had to do this? Then there would be only a nickel left for the trip home.

It wouldn't matter. Jim would be with her. They would walk home together. She would tell him about the big school and about Straw Hair.

Susan closed the book and looked at the clock. Father looked at it too. They laughed.

"Already we are becoming like the white man," Father said. "The clock tells us what to do. Now it says, 'go to sleep!'"

Susan yawned. She would need sleep tonight for

her long trip tomorrow. She crawled into her blanket roll near the kitchen door, tucking the map book safely under her head. When she held her hands in front of the blinking Used Car lights she could see a slim new moon in the black sky.

"It is a yellow canoe," she thought, "and Jim is poling it through the sky."

Morning came with the sound of horns and screeching brakes. Susan's heart ached for the morning song of a bird — even the blackbird's caw. But there was only the distant wail of a siren — which Father said blew because there was a fire — and the grating smash of metal in the car lot below.

The hard cover of the map book jabbed her neck. The book told of birds in Lincoln Park! Susan tossed the blanket aside, and rolled it against the wall. She must get everything ready for her trip!

Mother padded about the kitchen in her soft moccasins, unwrapping bread that Father had brought from the grocery store. Her heavy shawl hung about her shoulders.

"It is not cold, Mother," Susan said. "Why do you wear the shawl?"

"It is to shut out the city, Little Flower," Mother answered. "It is to crawl into the wigwam when there is a storm."

Susan understood. She had wanted a shelter at the

great brick school yesterday. She listened for Father, but there was only the padding sound of Mother's moccasins.

"Father," she called into the room that was always dark.

Mother interrupted, "I forgot to tell you, Susan. He left early for the grocery store. There was extra work."

Susan was relieved. She did not want to lie to him and pretend that she was going to the school. Now she would not turn to the right when she walked out of their apartment door. She would go in the other direction, to the thick black street called North Avenue on the map.

She promised Mother she would hurry home and then ran down the stairs and out the apartment door. She squeezed the map book tightly in her hand and pressed her foot against the bottom of her shoe, where she had put the coins Father gave her for lunch. She must not lose them.

She walked close to the windows of the stores so the fast-moving people wouldn't bump her. The windows flipped by like pages in a picture book. Each one was different. Fat sausages draped up and down in one of them like hooked-together tails of little pigs hung up to dry. Beside them was a window piled with leather bags.

"There is enough leather in this window," Susan thought, "for Father to make bright moccasins for every person at Lac du Flambeau."

A bearded man sat at a table in the window of the next store. He dipped a heavy doughnut in a cup of coffee. The smell of coffee floated through the open door.

A strange hurt came to Susan's throat. Grandmother always boiled coffee in the morning. At home on warm days in the fall, the smell of coffee mixed with the scent of pine needles was more delicious to breathe than beef boiling in the soup kettle.

Susan began to wonder if there would ever be an end to the stores. Her feet ached in the heavy shoes. Why not take them off? She could walk faster in bare feet. No one would notice. The people on the side-walk looked ahead with stiff eyes that did not move. She saw a green metal bench near the walk and sat on it.

The first shoe off clattered onto the cement, spilling the coins with a hurried tinkle. Susan grabbed them and stuffed them into the toe of the shoe. She spread her bare feet on the cool cement and smiled. City people would not look so stiff, she decided, if they walked in bare feet. She studied the crisscross streets on the map. She had only crossed half of them and the sun already shone from the top of the sky. She tucked her shoes and map book under her arm and started walking again. She would have to take the bus after all.

A busy, clanging street appeared before her. Cars and buses pushed and honked at one another. Green and red lights blinked off and on. People crowded the walks. Susan looked at the street sign. It was North Avenue. This was where she must take the bus. A large, fat yellow one stopped in front of her. The sign on the front said Lincoln Park!

Susan had only time to shake the money from her shoe and climb up the steps, where a Negro driver sat behind a big wheel and waited for people to slip their money into a little machine. A bell clanged and that was all. A fat woman shoved Susan along the aisle of the bus. All the seats were filled, but the standing people packed together like fish in a little bucket of water.

The bus started! It chugged and jerked. But it was impossible for Susan to fall because of the walls of people all around her. The bus driver began calling the names of streets. The walls of people jolted and the bus stopped. People shoved and pushed to get off and on. Susan wondered how she would ever squeeze through the people when she heard the bus driver call her stop.

The stop came sooner than she expected. "Lincoln

Park!" a deep voice shouted from the front of the bus.

A door near her slid open and most of the passengers stepped out. Susan followed. The people scattered down many sidewalks and the bus drove away. Susan was alone. In her mind she had thought the park would be small. She thought she would find Jim at once. Instead, there were chains of trees with sidewalks going through them in more directions than a sandpiper's tracks on the muddy beach of Rice Lake at home.

Where should she go? Where would she find the lake where Jim fished and built his fires? She looked beyond the trees and saw a world of blue clear water. She knew at once that it was Lake Michigan. She ran toward it. The water swished against the shore in steady waves that curled into white bubbles along the sand. People splashed in the waves and swam into the lake. Susan wanted to dive into the swelling water with them. Someday she would come here with Jim. They would take Mother from the dark hole of their house and Father from his worry about the clock and bring them to this water. Now she must find Jim.

She turned back on one of the sidewalks. A thunderous roar came from the row of trees in front of her. Susan jumped back, scattering her shoes, the money, and her map book in all directions. She looked about. None of the other people around her were frightened.

A little boy pulled his mother's hand and cried, "Let's watch the lion!"

Susan remembered. In the map book there was a page about wild animals in cages at the zoo. She wanted to see the lion too. She followed the boy and his mother until they came to a crowd of people gathered in front of a small iron cage. A great yellow beast stalked back and forth inside it, roaring at the people. His strong legs moved with the sureness of an Indian chief. This was the first time Susan had seen the animal of her totem. She was proud that her Father's totem had such a noble symbol.

A lumbering black bear, who lived in a cage across from the lion, sat on his haunches and reached through the bars for a tiny peanut. Susan wished she could buy a sack of peanuts for him. But she had only a nickel.

The nickel! It was gone! So were the shoes and the book with the map.

"I dropped them when the lion roared," Susan remembered.

She looked behind her. Which of the sidewalks had she followed? They all looked alike.

She must find Jim now. She could never walk home alone without the map. Her bare feet were dusty and hot. The largest crowds of people were in front of the animal cages. Jim liked animals. He might be watching them now. If she stood in front of the people, she could look back into every face.

In front of her a snow white bear lifted its shaggy body on its hind legs, weaving back and forth along the bars of the cage. Little boys and girls pulled their mothers toward the cage. Men and women crowded in front of the great beast. The bear towered above everyone. Jim might be here. Susan tried to push between the arms and shoulders of the crowded people. No one moved. Perhaps if she crawled on her hands and knees she could get to the fence and look back into their faces. She bent down. She wished she had shoes. No one else was barefoot. A heavy brown work shoe almost smashed her foot. She crawled away just as it shifted position.

Without warning, a rasping voice screeched above the crowd. "Stand up, girl! Stand up, girl! Stand up, girl!"

Susan stood up. She was terrified. She ran from the bear cage in the opposite direction and almost hit a long bar separating her from a finely wired pen. Inside a great green bird with an orange curved beak, blinkingly surveyed her. The shrill words, "Stand up, girl! Stand up, girl!" came from its throat. Uncle John had told her there were no evil spirits. Susan wondered. What could be inside a bird to make it talk?

12

Susan decided she would hunt for Jim where there were no animals in cages. She followed another sidewalk to a small blue pond that floated beneath a willow tree. Three children sat on its bank, tossing popcorn onto the water. A fat white duck bobbed up and down eating it. Susan stood shyly under the tree, wishing she had a box of popcorn for herself. She was hungry enough to build a fire and eat the duck.

A strange inner excitement made Susan tremble. The small quiet lake provided fish. The dead branches from the willow would make wood for a fire. The little curved bridge behind the nearby bushes would be shelter from rain. The willow tree with its low sweeping limbs could hide anyone in the top branches.

There were patches of burned grass near the water. Jim was here! Susan could feel his presence.

"Jim," she called suddenly.

Her voice disturbed the peaceful lake. The fat duck sailed away in the opposite direction. Shouting their disappointment, the children chased it along the shore, throwing all of their popcorn into the water. Soon they disappeared down a distant path.

Susan was afraid to call again. One voice in this silent spot could be heard as clearly as the lion's roar in the zoo. A fat policeman sauntered along the sidewalk and crossed the bridge, swinging a short club from his hand. Susan hid behind the sturdy trunk of the great tree.

"Little Flower." A husky whisper came from the branches above her.

Susan jumped. The whisper belonged to Jim!

The policeman stopped at the foot of the bridge as though the whisper had been directed at him. Susan was afraid to move. She cautiously leaned her head back and looked up. Jim's face poked out between the drooping branches. He pressed one finger against his lips. With his other hand, he pointed to the policeman. Susan leaned against the tree trunk. Jim wanted her to wait until the policeman moved away. He was hiding from him. She had found Jim, but they must be careful. The policeman must not take Jim. She would wait until he walked away. Then Jim could run with her through the park to North Avenue. It would not take long to find the apartment building on Clark Street if Jim were with her. They would surprise Mother and Father. Mother would cry with joy. Susan could hardly wait.

The policeman began walking toward the zoo.

"Little Flower," Jim called, this time in his normal voice. "Climb up the tree."

Susan caught the lowest limb and swung herself off the ground. It was simple to climb a willow. The limbs were smooth, and they branched out evenly like the prongs on a ladder.

Jim held his hand toward her. She grabbed it and he pulled her into the higher limbs where they were completely hidden by the thin sweeping leaves.

Both of them laughed. Jim had changed a little. His clothes were ripped and torn, but he was clean and he didn't look hungry. His hair was long and hung over his ears, but it was combed.

"You have the nose of a fox, Little Flower," Jim smiled. "How could you track me down in a city that is a giant? I have been hiding since yesterday."

"There is a story in the newspapers," Susan explained quickly, "about a boy who cooks fish in Lincoln Park. Someone thinks they saw him and that he is an Indian boy."

"In the newspapers?" Jim was incredulous.

He snapped his fingers knowingly. "That is what

the policeman meant yesterday, Susan. I heard him talk above me when I sat under the bridge. 'The newspaper stories are making a joke out of me,' the policeman said to a friend. 'They say I can't catch the boy who steals in the park.'"

"Do you steal the fish, Jim?" Susan was alarmed.

Jim held his head erect like Father when he talked at the Tribal Council meeting. "I do not steal, Susan. I take only what I can eat. I would starve without the fish. All of my money is gone."

"Of course," Susan agreed instantly.

Jim became worried. "If there is a story in the newspapers — there will be more than one policeman to look for me. I must leave Lincoln Park. It is not a good place to live now."

"We will leave now, Jim." Susan began climbing down the branches. "We will go home and surprise Mother and Father. There will be food from Father's grocery store. You can sleep on the little porch where the lights blink away the darkness of the night."

Jim grabbed her arm and pulled her into the branch beside him.

"Susan, you must listen to me and try to understand." His voice was urgent. "I do not want to run away from you and Mother and Father, but I must."

Susan was frightened. Jim talked as though he weren't going home with her.

Jim shifted restlessly into a high branch. Susan followed him. For a moment he relaxed.

"It isn't hard to live in such a park in the city," his dark eyes twinkled. "The big Lake Michigan has enough water for everyone in the world to swim. The little ponds are filled with fish. One night I ate a duck."

Susan thought of the fat white duck paddling now in the blue pond beneath them. She wished again that she could eat it.

Jim's lips pinched into the bitter look that Susan remembered from his last days on the reservation. "If I get caught here, I will be put in a jail."

"That's why we must hurry and go home, Jim." Susan became impatient. The policeman was not in sight. The children were gone. No one would see them slide down the tree.

Jim pounded one of the branches with his fist. "I can't go home with you. I'm sick of being an Indian and always being poor. I've got a job, Susan, washing windows on high buildings. The man who hired me yesterday has a truck. Next week I will work in a city in Minnesota."

"But Jim," Susan pleaded, "you must tell Mother and Father. You must go home with me now."

"They would never let me take this job." Jim threw his strong shoulders back and breathed deeply. "They want me to go back to Lac du Flambeau for one more year. I'm not going to be an Indian any more, Susan.

I'm going to change my name. I'm not coming back to Mother and Father until I can buy all the things that I want and all the things that you need."

"But I don't need much, Jim." Susan was bewildered. Tears came to her eyes. "How can you change your name and not be an Indian? Then you would not be my brother."

The bitterness disappeared from Jim's face. He smiled at Susan with affection.

"I will always be your brother, Little Flower." He took a cherished pocket knife from a chain on his belt and turned it over in his hand. "You take this knife. It's a present from me. Someday I'm going to give you a lot of presents."

Susan reached for the knife, uncertain what to do with it. Jim had never given her such a valuable gift.

A rustling beneath the tree silenced them. They stood motionless, moving only their eyes. Below them was the helmeted head of the large policeman. He had come back and they hadn't seen him. He sauntered about the tree trunk swinging his wooden club. Then he stopped abruptly and looked into the branches.

Susan stopped breathing. She could see his red face and bright blue eyes. Could he see them through the drooping leaves? Had she and Jim climbed high enough to disappear from the eyes of those on the ground? The policeman lowered his head and walked

117

to the bushes beside the pond, swishing his club through them.

"He's looking for me," Jim moved his lips without making a sound, but Susan could understand. "As soon as he leaves, Susan, I've got to run. I've got to get to that job tomorrow."

Susan nodded. Her heart thumped wildly. She didn't want the policeman to catch Jim.

Jim hesitated for a moment as though he might change his mind.

"Susan, I must know the address where you live. I will write a letter when everything is going good for me."

Susan reached into her pocket and gave Jim the paper with the address of their apartment on it.

"I didn't ask about Mother and Father." Jim hesitated again. "Is it hard for them in the city?"

"It is hard for them, and it is hard for me," Susan answered slowly. Maybe if they talked some more Jim would change his mind and stay.

The policeman disappeared.

"Susan." Jim's voice was commanding and sharp. "Promise not to tell Father and Mother about our meeting. I don't want them to try to find me. I have to do this."

A promise could not be broken. How could she promise not to tell Mother and Father that Jim was well and that he was not hungry. Susan's mind whirled in circles. She could not lie to them about her trip to Lincoln Park.

"It is a hard promise," Jim said.

Susan nodded.

"If I say, 'promise until I write a letter,' then it is not forever."

Jim was right and he had given her his knife to promise that he would always be her brother. She thought of Jim going back to Lac du Flambeau. It would be winter soon and there would be no job for him there.

"I will promise, Jim," Susan said solemnly.

Jim smiled. He tied his blue jacket around his waist and climbed noiselessly down the tree. When he reached the ground he looked up and waved hastily to Susan. Then he ran in a direction away from the pond.

Susan wanted to shout for him to come back. But she couldn't. The policeman might hear her.

She looked into the sky and saw the sun sliding toward the west. The afternoon would soon be ended. She had to find her apartment building before it got dark.

There had been no time to tell Jim that she had lost her map and that the address she had given him was many streets away.

13

Loneliness wrapped about Susan like a mist, and the hurt of losing Jim was a knife cut in her heart. She dreaded climbing down the tree and walking in the park again. But she must. When the sky became dark and she was not at home, Mother would wrap her shawl about her head and weep. Father would stride through their dark house like a lion caged in the zoo.

Through the leaves of the tree, Susan saw the sun moving swiftly toward the west. She slid quickly down the willow trunk and ran to the nearest sidewalk. The policeman was not in sight. She could hear the lion's shaking roar, so she followed the sound. A stone bench near the lion's cage was empty. Maybe if she sat on it and looked around she could remember where she lost her shoes, the money, and her map book. A fat woman with a sticky baby sat down beside her. The baby reached out and yanked Susan's hair. It didn't hurt much, but it added to the hurt that was every place — in her feet, in her head, and in her heart. Tears began to roll down her cheeks and she couldn't stop them.

The fat woman turned toward her.

"Well," she scowled, "the baby didn't pull that hard. What's the matter with you — no shoes and tangled hair."

The woman stared at Susan. "Say," she exclaimed, "you must be some kind of foreigner." She grabbed her baby around the waist and left.

Susan tried to smooth her hair and wipe the tears from her face. But she couldn't stop crying, and there was no place to go where people wouldn't stare at her. She covered her face with her hands.

A great voice boomed out at her.

"What's the matter, are you lost?"

Susan looked up with horror. The big policeman who had peered into the tree for Jim stood before her. His round stomach heaved up and down when he breathed and the brass buttons covering his uniform glistened in the sun like flashing cat's eyes. Susan could not look into his face.

Would he arrest her? Would he put her in jail? She had no shoes. It might be a crime in the city not to wear shoes.

"You're an Indian girl, aren't you?" His voice boomed again.

Susan nodded. Did he hate Indians like the fat lady with the sticky baby seemed to do?

"Where do you live, child?" he asked.

Susan reached in her pocket. The paper with the address on it was gone. She had given it to Jim, and she couldn't remember the number.

"I don't know," she answered weakly.

"Did you run away from school?"

Susan hesitated and then nodded again.

Maybe he punished boys and girls who ran away from school.

"Well," he said.

Susan saw him pull a little book from his pocket and begin to write in it.

"I have some friends at the American Indian Center," he said. "I'll put you in a taxi and send you over there. Come along with me."

He sounded like he was going to help her. Susan raised her eyes and looked into his face. It was round and red with kind blue eyes.

Susan followed him, unable to say a word. They walked to a busy street where he waved to a yellow taxi. When it stopped in front of them, he gave the driver a slip of paper and some money and helped Susan into the back seat.

"From now on you better stay in school on week

days," he said, and smiled and shook his finger at her.

Susan wanted to smile too, but she couldn't. She did whisper, "Thank you," before the taxi swerved away.

Susan grabbed the handle on the side door of the taxi to keep from sliding over the slippery cushions. The driver lurched into a stream of speeding cars. Susan closed her eyes and listened for them to crash. They didn't. Instead, the taxi slipped through the traffic as easily as a canoe gliding through stalks of wild rice grass. Susan was breathless when the car stopped.

"You're to go into that building, Miss," the driver said, pointing to a two-story building on the corner of a busy street. "And give the people in there this piece of paper."

He swung the door open for Susan, handed her the paper, and drove away.

Susan hesitated before the open door of the building that led up a steep flight of stairs. This building wasn't as tall as the place where Running Tongue worked. Would the people inside help her find Clark Street and the Bearskin apartment? At Running Tongue's building, Mother and Father had been with her. Now she was alone. She would have to tell someone inside what she had done. She had never talked to a white person. She had only asked and answered questions. Susan wondered if she should run away again and try to find her street alone. She glanced around her. This street was like all the others, with shops and signs and crowds of people. She felt like a spinning whirlpool without direction.

Susan turned and walked slowly up the stairs.

"Hello," a soft voice called.

Susan looked up. Standing above her was a tall, young Indian woman. Proud beauty shone from her deep brown eyes and finely shaped mouth. She had Grandmother's face without wrinkles!

"An Indian princess," Susan thought, remembering an ancient Chippewa legend. The woman's long black hair curled softly around her shoulders and brushed against the bright red of her clean new dress.

Susan handed her the paper from the taxi driver.

The lady read it quickly and smiled.

"My name is Mary Cloud." She took Susan's hand and led her into a small room with a desk and two green covered chairs. Other Indian men and women passed them in the hallway.

Pictures of Indians and newspaper clippings about Indians hung on the walls of the room. A large sign told of an Indian Pow Wow in Chicago. In one picture, an Indian basketball team posed in uniforms. All of the players lived in Chicago.

"Your building is a place for Indians in Chicago," Susan spoke suddenly.

Mary Cloud agreed. "I will tell you about the

American Indian Center later Now you must tell me your name, where you live, and why you ran away from school today."

Susan leaned against the soft arm of the chair. She was tired and hungry, but no longer afraid. Miss Cloud was an Indian.

"I went to Lincoln Park today because I thought my brother Jim was there. He —" Susan stopped. She couldn't tell about Jim. Jim didn't want anyone to know where he was.

Miss Cloud remained silent.

"I got lost," Susan continued. She told about the policeman and the speeding taxi.

Miss Cloud listened. All the words Susan had saved for Jim tumbled from her lips. She couldn't stop them.

"Our house is dark like a tunnel, Miss Cloud. The stove has a secret flame that we can't find, and Father watches the clock all the time. He says it is a god to the white man."

Susan talked on about the big school, Straw Hair, and Running Tongue.

Miss Cloud began writing in a book. She leaned forward when Susan mentioned Running Tongue.

"Your Running Tongue is a friend of mine," she laughed. "I must call her now on the telephone and get the address of your apartment building."

She walked to another room, but Susan could hear her low, confident voice.

"I wish our Indian people would ask for more help when they come to the city," she said. "If an Indian from our Center could visit them as soon as they arrive, we could answer questions that they would never ask a white person."

Susan was surprised. Miss Cloud talked to Running Tongue as though it didn't make any difference that she was an Indian.

The receiver clicked.

"We'll go to my house for a minute, Susan," Mary Cloud said, as she came back into the room. "Then I'll take you home. Your parents will be worried about you."

Mary Cloud threw a soft white sweater around her shoulders. It matched her spotless white shoes.

She is the Tallest Pine Trimmed with Fresh Snow, Susan decided.

Susan and Miss Cloud hurried down the stairs to a small gray car. Miss Cloud slid behind the wheel. Susan marveled that an Indian woman could drive a car. Father and Mother did not know how. Miss Cloud's long slim fingers turned the steering wheel as easily as Father guided his pole over the lake when fishing. She tossed a black shining strand of hair from her face and looked straight ahead as she began to talk.

"I was your age, Susan, when I came to Chicago. It wasn't easy going to school, and then finding a job when I finished. I have learned to live in this white man's city. But I am proud that I am an Indian. I visit my Sioux reservation in Minnesota at least once every summer."

She talked on. "You must stay in school, Susan, like I did. Listen to your teacher and read all of your books. Someday you will be moved to a grade with boys and girls who are the same size as you."

"Oh," Susan exclaimed. "I thought I would always be with the little children."

Miss Cloud laughed.

"Don't worry too much about Straw Hair," she continued. "He will tire of his Indian game with you. When recess comes, go to the part of the school ground where only the girls play."

Miss Cloud slowed the car and parked before a red brick building. Smooth round evergreens bordered the sidewalks and green blankets of grass spread beside them. Susan and Mary Cloud climbed three flights of stairs. Along the wall, wide windows opened to the light and little boxes beneath them glowed with red geraniums. Miss Cloud stopped before a tall brown door and twisted her key in the lock. Susan stepped inside.

"Oh!" Susan cried. "I didn't know houses could be so beautiful on the inside!"

To Susan the rooms were yellow sun, shining at noon in the middle of Rice Lake. They were red campfires, flickering over the faces of the dancers at the Rice Harvest. Bright Indian rugs covered the floors and the chairs of Mary Cloud's house. On the walls were paintings of Indians sitting around a campfire and paddling over a lake in a canoe. In one corner of the room was a drum like Father played for the dances at home. Along another wall were rows of books. All of them were about Indians.

"It is a wigwam in the city!" Susan cried.

Miss Cloud smiled as she hurried about her small kitchen, putting jars and boxes into a basket.

"I will bring you here again, Susan, when we can stay longer. Now, we must hurry to your house. It's getting dark and your parents will worry."

Susan lingered at the door. "Maybe someday I can live in such a house," she said.

Then her eyes brightened with a new exciting thought. "Why couldn't our houses on the reservation look like this, Miss Cloud?"

"They could, Susan." Miss Cloud's voice matched the excitement in Susan's.

Susan and Mary Cloud ran down the steps, which were lighted now with electric bulbs, and climbed into the car. Miss Cloud knew where to turn on the busy road. She raced through the streets with green lights and halted for those that were red. They had only driven a few blocks when Susan saw the Used Car sign behind her building.

"I live there!" she exclaimed, pointing toward the gray building. Miss Cloud slowed the car and backed into a parking space.

A group of people were huddled together in front of Susan's building. She saw Mother and Father and Running Tongue among them! A white cloth was wrapped around Mother's forehead.

"Mother!" Susan shouted. She opened the car door and raced across the street.

Mother welcomed her with outstretched arms. Father stood close by.

"It is good you have come home, Little Flower," he said fervently.

Mary Cloud and Running Tongue greeted one another as friends.

"Oh Mary," Running Tongue said with her breathless speech that tonight was faster than usual, "these people had a rock thrown through one of their windows tonight. . . . Mrs. Bearskin was cut on the head with broken glass. . . . The landlord says some of his tenants don't want Indians living in the building. . . . Then Susan didn't come home, and I wouldn't have known where to find her if you hadn't called from the Indian Center. . . . I just got here."

A short, red-faced man beside her said, "If having Indians in the building is going to cause trouble, then they better leave."

A man standing beside him slapped him on the

back and muttered, "We don't want Indians causing trouble around here."

Running Tongue turned upon both men with a torrent of words. Susan understood only part of them. She talked of "leases . . . breaking the law . . . landlords being arrested . . . high rents that rob the tenants."

Mary Cloud walked away from the red-faced man to look at the cut on Mother's head. Father's face was grim. He squeezed Susan's hand in his and stood facing the short man.

"I have not caused trouble in this building and I have paid my rent," he said. Susan was proud of the strength in Father's voice.

The short man, whom Susan decided must be the owner of the building, was now bowing and nodding to Running Tongue. He seemed to curl in like a timid snail. "I will put in a new window tomorrow," he said. "Of course, keeping peace in the neighborhood is something we all believe in." He backed away from them.

Running Tongue shook hands with Father and Mary Cloud. She waved to Susan and Mother and disappeared into the dark street.

A great gnawing question began to grow in Susan's mind. It had started like a tiny spider web at school when Straw Hair said he didn't want an Indian in his room. It had grown at the park when the mother pulled her sticky baby away because Susan was a "foreigner," which must have meant Indian. Now the web was big and tangled around her. Why did someone break their window? Why did the landlord say he didn't want Indians in his building?

The little band of people moved away. Even the landlord disappeared; only Mary Cloud was left. She walked with Mother, Father, and Susan up the dark stairs to their apartment. Father unlocked their door and pressed the button that spread light over the dark room with the bulging furniture. The jagged hole in the broken window snarled like the mouth of a fox. Sharp bits of glass pierced the floor.

Mother noticed Susan's bare feet.

"Little Flower, without shoes you will cut your feet on such a floor," she cried.

Father lifted Susan in his strong arms and carried her to the kitchen. He kicked the glass angrily aside with his foot. A red ball-like object rolled over the floor. Mary Cloud picked it up.

"This is the rock that broke your window," she said, unwrapping a red bandana handkerchief tied around a sharp white stone. "There is an *E* in the corner of it. The owner of this could be sent to jail."

An *E* on a red bandana handkerchief! Susan gasped, but remained silent. Straw Hair wore a bandana like this on his head. She had seen him in their building. Could he have broken their window? Susan bit her lip to keep from talking.

Mother and Father didn't know Straw Hair. Miss Cloud said to stay away from him. Maybe there were many bandanas with an *E* in the corner. How could she say this one belonged to Straw Hair? Did she want to tell and have this boy go to jail?

In the kitchen, Miss Cloud began washing Mother's head and rubbing medicine on it from a little bottle that she carried in her pocketbook. She talked quietly as she worked, telling them that she was a Sioux from Minnesota — that she had come to the city many years ago to work in the home of white people. Now she had a job as a social worker at the American Indian Center.

Susan began to feel weak. She sank to the floor and leaned against the wall.

"Little Flower," Mother looked at her with alarm. "We thought only of the broken glass and my cut. What has happened to you?"

"I am hungry, Mother," was all Susan could say.

Mother brought a glass of milk and more crackers.

"There is no more food," Father said. "All the money I had today was paid to the landlord for rent."

Mary Cloud picked up her basket and placed it on the table.

"Tonight we will have a feast," she announced. "I

am going to show Mrs. Bearskin how to light this gas stove. Then we will cook dried corn and turnips, dried beef and dried apples." She searched through her basket. "There is coffee too!"

Mother's face brightened. She laid an Indian blanket on the floor beside the stove. "We will sit on it like we do at home," she laughed.

Susan laughed with her. She couldn't understand why she did. Her day had been filled with dark shadows. The jagged glass on the living room floor — the ugly rock with the red bandana around it — the cold loneliness of Lincoln Park — were nightmares to remember. She couldn't tell anyone about Jim, and he hadn't come home with her; but, she had found an Indian friend for herself and for Mother and Father.

14

THE EARTHY FRAGRANCE of Indian food lingered in the Bearskin kitchen long after Mary Cloud's feast ended. Mother's coffeepot bubbled above the blue flame that burned without wood.

Susan told the story of Straw Hair and Lincoln Park, but she could not talk about Jim. Even if she had not made the promise, how could she say that Jim did not want to be an Indian?

"If the boy you call Straw Hair is telling the truth," Father said, "it could be our Jim who cooked fish in the park."

Susan was silent. Straw Hair was telling the truth. Jim did cook fish in the park. Her thoughts were so clear, Susan wondered why everyone in the room couldn't hear them.

Mary Cloud interrupted. "You must not wander around the city alone, Susan. When you want to look for your brother, you must promise to tell me."

Susan hesitated. Could she keep another promise? This one would not be hard. She had already promised not to tell about Jim or to look for him.

"Yes, I will promise," she said finally.

It was late when Miss Cloud began packing her basket to leave. She arranged to come for Mother the next day and take her to the Indian Center. Susan stood beside her, sick in her heart with a question that had to be asked.

"Why did the landlord say that people don't want Indians living in this building?" Susan's voice trembled. "Why did someone break our window tonight?"

Mary Cloud lifted her head. A cascade of shining black hair fell over her shoulders. Her high cheek bones cast shadows under her dark, serious eyes.

She must be the daughter of an Indian chief, Susan thought.

Mary Cloud spoke softly. "Dislike of the Indian started long ago, Susan. Many early settlers who came to America were greedy for land. They did not understand that Indians lived on the land and used it, but did not believe in owning it. The white settlers took this land. They broke the Indian's spirit and destroyed his means of making a living. Since that time our people have been pushed around until they feel inferior. They are untrained for jobs in this modern world, and they are always poor."

She talks like Uncle John, Susan thought.

"Today, Susan, many white people like Running Tongue are our friends. But there are still some who cling to the old ideas. They do not like anyone who is different."

Mary Cloud paused and looked directly at Susan.

"It is important for some Indians to become successful in the white man's world so the others will not be without hope. This is why you must go to school, Susan. Without education, Indians cannot succeed in the city, and they cannot find a better way of life on the reservations."

Mother and Father nodded.

Mary Cloud glanced at Father's clock.

"If I don't go home now," she exclaimed, "the night will soon be over. All of us have a busy day tomorrow."

She waved a hurried good-bye and disappeared down the dark stairway.

Susan had forgotten about tomorrow. Mary Cloud's visit was like going home. Now she must think of Straw Hair and the school . . . and she had no shoes!

She could not go in bare feet. Dangling on a nail above her blanket roll were her moccasins. Of course, they would be her shoes for school until the winter came.

The next morning when Susan walked out-of-doors with Father, her feet felt as though they were covered with feathers. Instead of the clomp of her heavy shoes on the hard cement, the moccasins made no sound at all. They were as good for the city streets as for the paths of the forest.

Father left her at the corner, with his face worn with wrinkles and his back hunched with burdens. At home on the reservation, not even the winter winds bent his back. There he stood as straight as the trunk of the pine tree.

Almost a block from the school, Susan saw Straw Hair pacing in circles at the edge of the school ground. He was dragging a small boy behind him and pushing him against a light pole.

"He's hurting the little boy."

Susan became angry. She ran to the school ground and stood in front of Straw Hair.

"Stop hurting that little boy," she cried.

Straw Hair swung around and grinned.

"Look who's here," he shouted, motioning to all the

little boys to gather around him. "It's the big Indian!"

Susan looked straight into his narrow blue eyes.

"You should stop hurting little boys and you should stop throwing rocks into people's windows." Susan felt her knees tremble and heard her heart thump. She had not meant to say anything about the rock.

Straw Hair scowled, "What do you mean, throw rocks in your window?"

"I saw a handkerchief like yours tied around a rock that went through our window last night." Susan did not move, even though Straw Hair shoved his face near hers and clenched his fist.

"Prove it!" he shouted. Then he looked down at her feet.

"Moccasins," he yelled, bending over and laughing loudly.

"Why do you want to wear lousy old moccasins; you might as well go bare-footed. Why don't you put feathers on your head too?"

A group of boys and girls gathered near them in a tense circle. No one joined Straw Hair's laughter.

Susan twisted the ring on her finger. This was the time to think about Indians having courage.

"Father made these moccasins," Susan said proudly, looking down at her feet. "He makes the best moccasins on our reservation."

"Reservation!" Straw Hair jeered. "Do you know what a reservation is?" His big body swung around the little boys huddled in a circle. "It's a place where the government keeps lazy Indians and feeds them because they won't work."

The little boys remained silent.

Tears came to Susan's eyes.

She didn't know how to answer Straw Hair. The government did feed her people sometimes when they were starving. Many of the Indians didn't work, but it was because they couldn't find jobs.

"My father and my brother Jim are not lazy," Susan said, looking again into Straw Hair's eyes. She was surprised to find herself shouting.

She twisted the lion ring until it cut her finger.

"My father made these moccasins and they are better than your shoes," she shouted again. "They walk better and they run better."

"Run better!" Straw Hair clapped his hands against his stomach and bent over laughing. "I could beat you running with my shoes tied together."

"Then we will race," Susan announced. She had to say it. She must race for her tribe to show that they were not lazy. She would race to show that Chippewa moccasins were strong and made for running. Indians did not race to win for themselves. She would not win for herself.

The children in the circle around them became excited. "A race," they called to each other. "Earl is going to race the Indian girl."

Straw Hair slid his hands into the pockets of his tight brown pants. He swaggered through the group of children.

"I hate to waste my breath on a girl — especially an Indian."

He swung around and faced Susan. "But you asked for it. Don't say I didn't warn you."

A group of Earl's friends began pushing the circle along the racing area. Someone drew a starting and stopping line with a piece of chalk. Susan noticed that it was a long run. She bent down to tie the leather laces of her moccasins.

A teacher came striding toward the milling group of children. He pushed them aside until he stood beside Earl and Susan. Earl was startled but quickly grinned and bowed to the tall, young man. Susan thought she had never seen such a pale white man.

"Hello, Mr. Clark." Straw Hair spoke with surprising control and good manners. "This girl has challenged me to a race." He pointed to Susan.

Mr. Clark focused his attention on Susan's moccasins.

"Don't you want gym shoes?" he asked. He laced his fingers together and cracked his bony knuckles.

"No!" Susan answered at once. "That is why I race. It is to show that Chippewa moccasins are good for running."

Mr. Clark cracked his knuckles again. Susan wished he would stop. The sound made her stomach jump.

Straw Hair paced about, rolling up the sleeves of his plaid shirt. He nudged the little boys around him and winked in Susan's direction. Some of them laughed, but most of them were sober.

"You start the race, Mr. Clark," Earl said in his new, polite voice. "Then we can be sure that everything is fair and no one cheats."

Mr. Clark agreed and walked to the starting line. His bony fingers cracked as he shaded his eyes to survey the running area. He motioned for the boys and girls to move back from the line. Large groups of children had gathered now. Susan wondered if everyone on the school ground would watch the race. She did not want so many eyes staring at her.

Susan pressed the ring on her finger. She thought of Uncle John. He would understand why she was running.

Mr. Clark beckoned for Susan and Earl to come to the starting line. He bent down to check that both their feet were behind it. Susan glanced at the long race track of hard cement. She had only raced on the soft earth. Would her feet pound against this rock?

Her moccasins might not spring and carry her flying like the water swallow. What if Earl's shoes were meant for the city and hers would race only on the grassy earth?

Mr. Clark fumbled in his pockets for a whistle. There was a startling hush as he drew in his breath to blow. Susan thought of the tense quiet before a tornado that once struck the reservation.

Brrrrrrr! Susan dashed forward as though the shrill whistle had given her a push. Earl was beside her, running with his head down and his face steaming red. For a second they ran together, their arms swinging back and forth in unison. Then Susan felt Earl's body shoving against her. He was running crooked and pushing her into the line of boys and girls who screamed along their track. If she fell against them she would lose the race. She must drop behind Earl as he wove back and forth. There was no way to run around him without bumping his large body.

"Is this a new way to race?" Susan wondered, holding down her pace. If it was, she must find a way to dash through and then stay in front of this weaving boy.

A chant began to grow among the screaming bystanders.

"Come on, Earl. Beat the Indian girl. Come on, Earl. Beat the Indian girl."

It grew louder. The children began to clap their hands with the rhythm it made.

Soon they would reach the end of the line, where they would turn around and dash back to Mr. Clark. When they reached it, Earl put his foot on the line, almost crushing Susan's who came down beside it. He paused for a moment to pat the shoulder of one of his shouting friends. Susan saw that his face was shining with sweat. He was panting like Lame One after a swim in Rice Lake.

"He is running as fast as he can!" Susan realized.

This was her chance to dash ahead. Their feet were together on the chalk line. Earl could not push against her. Now she could run, swift and straight as the arrow from Jim's bow. Her moccasins sprang from the ground, carrying her through the air like the swallow.

Susan no longer heard the chanting. It had stopped. There were scattered cheers here and there through the crowd.

"Hurray for the Indian!" someone yelled close beside her.

Hurray for the Chippewa, Susan cheered to herself.

She could see Mr. Clark. His pale face was flushed. His twisted fingers cracked back and forth over his knuckles.

Susan's right moccasin came down on the finishing

line. A circle of children closed around her, shouting and whistling.

"Where is Earl?" Susan asked, looking behind her. He was far down the line. His heaving and panting could be heard above the cheering. He was walking toward her now swinging both his big arms.

Would he hit her? Susan forgot the race and her winning moccasins. Earl faced her. His eyes were puffed and red. His shoulders heaved up and down as though pumping for air.

The children began cheering for Susan.

"Rah! rah! rah! for the Indian girl!" someone yelled behind Mr. Clark. Others joined in the cheering.

Susan wasn't listening. All her attention was focused on Straw Hair.

His eyes shifted nervously over the crowd of children. No one gathered around him.

The school bell clanged! The cheering crowd began melting away into their lines.

For a moment Susan and Earl stood together. Earl moved uneasily away from her.

He is afraid when he is alone, Susan realized. He is the timid bear who only growls when he is with other bears. I will not be afraid of him again.

Then Earl looked at her moccasins.

"It's those moccasins that helped you win the race."

Susan nodded.

Earl squinted at them carefully.

"Say," he said, swaggering again with his hands in his pocket, "do you think I could buy a pair from your old man?"

Susan thought for a moment. Father could not make his beautiful moccasins because he had no money to buy the leather and the beads.

"If my father had money," she answered cautiously, "he could make you a pair of moccasins that would run as fast as the deer."

15

THAT EVENING Susan told Father and Mother about the race. Her eyes shone like sunshine on ripe blackberries.

Father laughed. Mother smiled. She had met Indian women at Mary Cloud's Indian Center, and her day had not been lonely.

"Straw Hair wants moccasins for his feet so they will run as swift as the deer. He will pay money for them." Susan was excited.

Father laughed again. "If this Straw Hair has a stomach that needs holding with two hands, he will need more than moccasins for racing like the deer. But if he will pay, I can buy new leather."

A loud banging sounded at their door.

"Maybe it is Mary Cloud," Susan brightened.

Father walked to the door and swung it open.

Susan gasped!

Straw Hair stood before them. The stubble of his hair was flattened to his head with a glistening paste. His blue eyes bulged with excitement. Their narrow cunning had disappeared. He held three one dollar bills in his hand.

"I am Earl Brown," he said in the polite voice he used for Mr. Clark on the playground. "My uncle is the landlord of this building. I live with him. I thought I could buy some moccasins from you."

Susan pinched her hands together. Would Father think of the *E* for Earl on the bandana? Would he get the handkerchief from the kitchen shelf where he put it last night and accuse Earl of breaking their window?

Susan looked at Father. His face was not angry. In fact, there was a slight smile on it.

"Come in," Father said to Earl. "My daughter told me that you wanted a pair of moccasins."

Straw Hair glanced at Susan briefly. "Hello," he said, then walked in and handed Father the money.

"Will this be enough money to make a pair of moccasins like your daughter has?"

Father stretched the bills in his hands.

"It will be enough," he answered. "Now you must sit in the chair while I measure your foot." Father opened a door on the kitchen cupboard and pulled out a box. Susan recognized it at once. It contained Father's tools for making moccasins. He placed it on the kitchen table. Earl sat beside him, fascinated by the contents.

Would Father let Earl touch the tools? Susan wondered.

Mother called her to the porch above the Used Car lot. She wanted to talk of Mary Cloud and the Indian Center. A cold wind swirled about their feet, blowing little scraps of dirty paper into noisy piles.

"It is the coming of winter," Mother said, pulling her shawl more tightly about her shoulders.

Susan wiggled her toes in the soft moccasins. They would not be warm enough for snow and ice. But she was glad she had worn them today at the school.

"I will tell you again about the race," she said to Mother, moving close to the warm shawl.

She forgot about Earl. When she turned around to look into the kitchen, Earl was holding one of Father's tools. His stubby hair had sprung loose from the paste and his face was a puffed red cherry. Father sat back in his chair, viewing the boy.

"It is enough for tonight that we have made the proper measurements," he said, putting the tools into the box. "Next week I will have bought the leather and the beads. Then you can come again."

Straw Hair looked quickly in the direction of Susan

and hesitated. Then he swaggered to the door. "I have paid for the moccasins. I better come and see how you make them."

Father rose from his chair and walked to the door with Earl. When he came back to the kitchen, Mother and Susan joined him.

"If the boy is busy, he will have no time for bad thoughts and bad play." Father rubbed his strong fingers over the tool box. "The boy, Earl, may be more clever with his hands than with his feet or his head."

Father pulled the red bandana with the *E* from his pocket. He spread it on the table.

"I think the *E* might be for Earl," he said to Mother and Susan.

A great worry lifted from Susan's mind. Now she could tell Father and Mother everything about Straw Hair.

They listened to her story. Father lit his pipe and puffed thin circles of smoke. This was the way he always prepared for the making of an important decision.

"I think the boy will not tease you again at the school, Little Flower," he said finally. "Someday I will ask him if the handkerchief belongs to him." He folded the bandana and carefully put it in a grocery sack on the shelf. "When that day comes, Straw Hair will forget that he did not like Indians."

Father pulled a chair under the kitchen light, which dangled on a cord from the top of the ceiling. Before sitting down, he drew a long crinkled envelope from the pocket of his blue jeans.

"It is from Striking Thunder," he said, "it came to me this morning at the grocery store."

"Is it about Jim?" Mother asked at once.

Jim! He had been on Susan's mind all through the day. It was not right that Mother and Father should think he was hurt or in trouble. But she had promised not to tell about their visit.

There had been no word from home since the Bearskins arrived in Chicago. Grandmother could read but she had never learned to write. Striking Thunder always sent the messages that were important and needed by the old people on the reservation.

Susan looked at the large, carefully written letters. She pictured Striking Thunder's steady hand, writing the words. His forehead would be furrowed with wrinkles and his eyes would pierce into the paper like flying arrows.

Father began to read: "Cold weather has come early to Lac du Flambeau. Many are sick and there is not enough food. Grandmother has wood for the fire and dried fish to eat. She will need money for bread and coffee and sugar. No one hears from Jim. Is he with you in the city?" It was signed, Striking Thunder.

There was silence in the room. Each of them felt the closeness of home and the needs of those they loved. Only Susan could answer the question about Jim.

Mother bowed her head and wiped her eyes with the fringe of her shawl.

"Our Jim is lost," she said. "There are as many places to look as stars in the sky. Where can we find him?"

Father folded the letter carefully and placed it in the box with his moccasin tools.

"Our Jim is strong and not afraid," he reminded Mother. "He is quick with his mind. He will not be gone long."

Susan was reassured. Jim was strong and clever. If he could cook fish in a park, he could take care of himself wherever he went.

16

THE SWIRLING LEAVES on the Bearskin's little porch the night Mother and Susan stood on it while Father talked with Straw Hair, had foretold of winter. Susan was glad for her warm blue coat that buttoned tightly under her chin. She would wear the moccasins until the coming of snow. By then Father would have saved money from the grocery store for a new pair of hard, thick shoes.

For many weeks now Straw Hair had come to their house to help Father make the moccasins. He would never talk with Susan in the apartment or at school.

"The boy is ashamed, Little Flower," Father said to her one evening. "And he is too proud yet to tell you." He paused, and then added, "Perhaps, it is enough that he is no longer a bully and a tease."

"It is enough," Susan smiled with gratitude.

"It would be good if the problem of Jim could be so easy," Father said, and his face creased into wrinkles of worry. Susan could see fear and despair in his eyes.

I cannot hold the secret much longer, Susan thought, pressing her hands tightly over her mouth to keep from talking.

A sharp rap shook their door.

It is Straw Hair, Susan thought, and shrugged her shoulders and walked toward the room where Mother and Father slept. Tonight she did not want to see him.

"It could be Jim," Mother whispered.

"It is not Jim," Father said. "It is the knock of a woman."

He went to the door.

It was a woman. It was Running Tongue.

She walked quickly into the kitchen, peering above her glasses at some peeling paint on the faded green wall.

"Considering all the money you pay for rent," she said rapidly, "this kitchen should be painted."

Running Tongue pulled off her gloves and stretched them out neatly on the table. Then she shook the creases from her coat and hung it over a chair. She pulled a letter from the pocket of her coat and placed it on the table.

"This letter was in your box downstairs," she said.

Mother, Father, and Susan leaned over the table to look at it. The handwriting was Jim's!

"It must be a letter from your son," Running Tongue interrupted. "I know you are worried about him. But let me talk with you just a moment before you open it." She paused long enough to wipe her glasses.

Mother leaned against the table. Father's hand tightened on her shoulder. Susan's heart began thumping like a tom-tom.

Why would Running Tongue bring news of Jim?

"I decided to stop here tonight on my way to a meeting. It is almost impossible to reach you on the telephone." Running Tongue pulled a long white envelope from her leather purse. It crackled as she took a letter from it.

Mother's hand trembled on the table.

"The Bureau of Indian Affairs has located Jim," Running Tongue said, as she quickly scanned the paper in her hand from top to bottom, as though deciding if she should read it aloud. Her decision was no. She placed the letter on the table and sat in the closest chair.

She glanced around the table at Mother, Father, and Susan and then focused her attention on Father.

"Your son is in the city of Minneapolis, Minnesota. He is well and safe."

Mother swayed slightly and Father helped her to a chair.

Running Tongue talked on. "He has a job, and he wants to change his name. He wants to be called Jim White."

"Jim White!" Susan couldn't understand. "Why does he like such a name better than Jim Bearskin?"

Susan turned her attention quickly back to Running Tongue. It was necessary to listen every minute or she would miss some words.

"Your Jim no longer wants to be an Indian. He wants to forget the reservation and he does not want you to contact him." Running Tongue emphasized each word in the last sentence. "Now I must leave so you can read his letter."

"No," Father said kindly. "You must stay. You are our friend."

He ripped the envelope open with his knife and slowly read aloud:

"Dear Mother and Father,

I am sorry you had to worry. Do not try to find me. I am well and I have a job, and I don't want to come back. If I want to live in the world of the white man, it is better not to have a Chippewa name. I am going to be Jim White, but I am still your son.

Someday I will own a big car — then I will take

all of you on a trip. I will buy Mother and Grand-mother a warm house. I will get Father tools for a shop. I will buy Little Flower many new dresses. Tell her that she can talk about our secret in the willow tree.

Your son,
Jim"

Everyone turned to Susan. Even Running Tongue did not speak. Susan sighed with great relief. The promise to Jim had been the hardest she had ever tried to keep.

"I found Jim in the park," Susan said simply. "He was hiding in a willow tree. I promised that I wouldn't tell."

"Well," was the only word Running Tongue could say.

Mother and Father were speechless.

"If you want my advice, here it is," Running Tongue said, as she began pulling her gloves over her long fingers. "Since the boy has a job, let him find his own way of life. Some Indians want to live like white men. Other Indians want to better their way of life on the reservation. Each should have the freedom to make his choice."

She glanced at her watch and hurried to the door. "I'll stop again tomorrow and get your decision," she

called. Her clipped steps could be heard, disap-
pearing down the stairs.

"Running Tongue is like the whirlwind," Father
said, standing with folded arms in front of the kitchen
door. He looked into the blinking lights of the Used
Car sign. "When she leaves it takes time for all that
she has said to settle."

He did not move for many minutes. Then he
walked onto the little porch and motioned for Mother
and Susan to follow. He looked above the sign to the
black sky dotted with yellow stars. He stood straight
and tall.

He is one of the leaders of our tribe, Susan thought
with pride, remembering how Father had stood above
the flaming firelight at the wild rice harvest and
praised the Great Spirit for the blessings of food.

"Our Jim is alive and has a job," Father said. "He
must decide for himself how he wants to be a man."

Mother was silent. Susan looked at the stars, blot-
ting out the jittering lights below. She remembered
Jim's strong shoulders and determined face when he
stood in the branches of the willow tree. He was becoming a man.

Father spoke again. "Running Tongue tells the
truth. Some of us choose to be Indians and want to
live on our reservations. We must hold our heads
high. We must be our own leaders and learn to sup-
port ourselves."

Susan slipped one hand between Father's strong fingers and held the fringe of Mother's shawl with the other one.

She knew that someday they would go home to Lac du Flambeau. Now there was much to learn in the city, and she had just begun to know Mary Cloud.

A bouncing light flashed on Uncle John's ring, outlining the strong head of the silver lion. Susan thought of the words Uncle John had said that day at the railroad station when he gave her the ring. A light flashed again on the lion's head.

"I promise," Susan whispered softly, "to always be proud that I am a Chippewa."